To Jo,

In Coal Blood

Best Wishes,

Geoff Green

JAN — 2014

IN COAL BLOOD

Geoff Green

Book cover reproduced from a photograph kindly provided by the Health and Safety Executive,
Health and Safety Laboratory, Harpur Hill, Buxton, Derbyshire.

Matador
9 Priory Business Park
Kibworth Beauchamp
Leicestershire LE8 0RX, UK
Tel: (+44) 116 279 2299
Fax: (+44) 116 279 2277
Email: books@troubador.co.uk
Web: www.troubador.co.uk/matador

ISBN 978-1783062-898

British Library Cataloguing in Publication Data.
A catalogue record for this book is available from the British Library.

Typeset in Aldine by Troubador Publishing Ltd
Printed and bound in the UK by TJ International, Padstow, Cornwall

Matador is an imprint of Troubador Publishing Ltd

For Betty – For Everything

In remembrance of my dear mother
May Green (née Elton)
and my dear father
Edward (Ted) (Cabba) Green, collier of Cossall Colliery,
located near Ilkeston Junction on the
Nottinghamshire/Derbyshire border.

Both born and bred in Cotmanhay, Ilkeston, Derbyshire.

PREFACE

I never thought that I would write this; my first novel. More than 20 years ago, I wrote a poem called 'ALL FOR COAL' – set in the coal mining industry – which I loved and which gave me my livelihood. *The poem has nothing to do with the story-line or the plot in this book.* It does, however, reflect the arduous life of many hundreds of thousands of coal face workers (colliers) who worked in coal mines over the centuries; and the dangers that prevailed. It also relates to the trauma felt by mining families when, over the years, thousands of fatal accidents occurred underground – many miles from expert medical help. The poem describes what it was like to be a collier when coal was won solely by hand. In that context, it dovetails into this novel. I thought I would record the poem here as some form of introduction to my novel; and as a token of my respect to all those associated with the coal mining industry here in the UK and around the world, both past and present.

Geoff Green

ALL FOR COAL

Frosty morning, peaked caps bobbing,
Hands in pockets, freezing cold,
Pit lane icy, footsteps dicey,
Miners walking, young and old.

Warm baths waiting, pit clothes drying,
Fusty smelling, hard and mould,
Lamp-room clattering, cap-lamps dangling,
Busy chattering, hearts of gold.

Shaft top clanging, cage gates lifting,
Men descending, stories told,
Coalface living, pit props creaking,
Shot-fire deafening, broken coal.

Conveyors running, shovels scraping,
Turning, flinging, loading coal,
Bodies glistening, steaming, sweating,
Blackening, tiring, muscles bold.

Roof top breaking, rock fall crashing,
Miners screaming, crushed with load,
Colleagues wrenching, digging, pulling,
Freeing, bleeding, saving goal.

Stretchers carrying, miners writhing,
Shocked and crying, broken, cold,
Pit-top waiting, family aching,
Doctors tending, dying souls.

Warm fires burning, lights all working, coal supplying,
Miners dying, widows crying,

Boys out playing,

Their turn next,
And all for coal.

PART ONE

(February 1938)

CHAPTER ONE

The alarm clock burst into life, the noise of its mechanical chattering accentuated by the linoleum floor and the starkness of the damp room. A weary hand draped from the bed and a finger groped for the knob that would kill the noise and puddle the brain in Joe's waking moment. It was 5.30am and freezing cold.

The bedroom was small and the second-hand bed had a dull, dark-brown lustred wooden frame, scratched randomly, and a distorted sprung mattress base, the springs fatigued in sympathy with its two occupants. There was a smattering of iced condensation on the inside of the small glass panes of the bedroom window and a dribble of condensation beneath the sill and part way down the dank wallpaper below. The relatively fresh cold air in the room was punctuated by the light smell of ammonia from the pot below the bed. The smell was lightly supplemented by semi-dried, sweaty bodily fluids that had smeared themselves onto private parts before the early night's intimate activity had induced sleep in the two occupants.

There was damp condensation on the top of the drab yellow quilt but a warmth beneath the sheets that held onto him for dear life. It pulled Joe's eyes closed and tried to dissuade him from any further movement. He could feel his wife's body spooned to his and he could sense the femininity of her smooth closeness. The testosterone build-up in the night was already inducing his brain to activate his desires, despite the cold tiredness of a new day. He had undergone this trial of wills a thousand times – being wakened before his sleep was out, knowing that he had to get up no matter how tired he was or what was creeping into his mind because of the proximity of his wife. There was a black pig-hole of a job waiting for him at the pit and he had to respond no matter what.

He moaned semi-subconsciously. His wife had also stirred.

'Joe.' A predetermined pause followed, then a little louder. 'Joe.'

'What?'

'It's time to get up.'

'I know.' It was a resigned retort that meant he did know. He had a duty to get up, a duty to the woman beside him and to the two sleeping kids in the next bedroom. His job, his efforts, his work, his pay, kept them with a roof over their heads and food in their bellies. There was little left over after that – but there were compensations. Mary was still unbelievably beautiful and the two children fit and healthy.

Joe forced himself sideways out of bed and placed a first reluctant foot onto the cold lino floor.

'Bloody hell!' he winced.

He grappled in near complete darkness for his matches and lit one with nocturnal expertise, then drooped it onto a candle wick sitting in a half-corroded enamel holder on the floor. The candle flickered into life and illuminated the bedroom with an orange-yellow bobbing light. There was enough light to see his underpants, socks, trousers and shirt lying damply on the floor waiting to be re-introduced to some form of body warmth. He dressed with drowsy expertise, glanced at his wife still in the warmth of their bed, grabbed the pullover from the door hook and pulled it over his head.

Joe blew out the candle, put the holder onto the floor and memorised his orientation to enable him to depress the latch on the thin bedroom door and pull it gently towards him. Trying not to induce any sound that might stir the children, he shuffled lightly onto the bare wooden landing, carefully placed his hand onto the handrail and guided himself down the cold wooden stairs in complete darkness. He pushed open the door at the bottom of the stairs and clicked the cold, brittle switch on the living room wall. The light bulb, dangling from a single twist cord in the centre of the room, glowed with a listless yellow-white tinge but was sufficient to enable him to close the door and cross the small living room to the small but functional kitchen. Joe lit another candle stub sitting in a holder on the box-board unit, twisted the knob on the simple gas ring, applied the same match to the lethal carbon monoxide hissing jet and placed a half-full kettle on top of the blue flame. Removing the kettle before it had time to whistle, he poured hot water into a dark blue teapot and stirred the leaves quietly. He made tea in a large ironstone mug, boasting a yellow flowered pattern, and sipped it gently and quietly. Placing the unwashed mug onto the simple kitchen unit, Joe took his thick but tired overcoat from the kitchen door hook, stuffed some cheese sandwiches he had made the night before, and had wrapped in greaseproof and newspaper, into one pocket, opened the back door and strode depressingly into the cold grey morning air. He walked quietly across the cobbled back yard and past the coal-house and outside toilet to his right. He unlatched a simple slatted wooden halfgate to his right, then turned right again and walked down an arched brick entry onto the slabbed pavement and cobbled road that connected fifty houses of the same ilk. The dullness of the morning hid the pride that had been taken with most of the house fronts. Doors wiped clean with elbow grease, and vigorously polished red-painted front stone steps, were examples of human female pride in an environment of surprising family stability amongst the reality of working-class poverty.

Joe was not alone on his street. There were other glimmers of light from other depressing windows and there were other shadowy figures huddling out onto the narrow street, illuminated by a single gas-light which had been manually lit at dusk the night before by a very old, wheezing gas-lighter man with a spindly wooden ladder and legs to match. All the shadowy figures were distinctly men; peak-capped, ratter-wearing men with hands in pockets except for those fingering a life-saving cigarette to a desperate mouth. Where they were going didn't allow for cigarettes.

Each man walked with a different gait. Some had a spring and youthfulness to them, others were strong and determined while others were bent with age and had an accompanying cough and a spit, still darkened by the coal dust they had inhaled the day before and from the years before. The trail from this street grew with others from other streets and, as the pit-head came into view, there was a steady stream of maleness dribbling itself forward for another challenging day. A day that would be in an all-male, dusty, noisy, sweaty, coal-blackened environment which, despite its abject grimness, provided an atmosphere of camaraderie and gutsiness, the like of which could not be seen anywhere else, except perhaps in the trenches.

Each man entered in turn the surface deployment centre and presented themselves to their respective bosses, the deputies. They placed a plastic badge from a master board onto a hook on a smaller board, overseen by their deputy, that signified their working place. Each deputy's board represented a specific location below ground, the specific deputy's district. Pit Bottom, Piper Seam 10's district, Piper 11's district, Low Main Seam 40's district, 39's salvage district, 42's development district. Also on the badge was their job title – coal face worker, packer, ripper, coal cutter, driller – a badge with a name and a particular expertise. By 6.30am, each deputy would know who had arrived and where they were to be deployed below ground. Any shortage would be made up with "bank colliers", often those who were not quite good enough to warrant a regular place, on a regular shift on a regular district.

Joe Murphy placed his tally on the board and nodded with quiet respect to his deputy Arthur Shelton.

'Good morning young fella, ready for another easy day, not been shagging all night again have ya?'

'Only half the night Arthur – she can't keep pace wi me.'

'You should send her round to our house then, there's life in th'old dog yet thi' knows.'

The slang was Derbyshire, nearly Nottinghamshire. Joe

7

respectfully responded that Mrs Shelton would not be too pleased about the proposed arrangement and the two men smiled at each other with a father and son warmth of a first joke of the day and a mutual respect. The deputy was the boss and he knew it, and he also knew that the workman was a first-class collier. The gruff, uncompromising but jokingly cynical exterior of these men hid from view the fact that only ball-achingly genuine hard work was good enough at this mine, coupled with the fact that their safety, and that of everyone else, down in the bowels of the earth, was paramount.

Joe migrated with all the other miners through to the clean side of the pit-head baths. He opened his clean locker, took out the soap in its holder – and a drab, crinkly dry towel – and took off his clean clothes and placed them in his locker. He walked bollock naked through to the dirty locker side of the baths carrying his soap and towel and his cheese sandwiches. He opened the dirty locker and put on his dirty but dry pit clothes. He placed the towel and soap into the dirty locker, twisted the key and stuck it into his pit trouser pocket. The cheese sandwiches were pushed down the front of his part-open shirt and then covered with a pullover. In his left hand he carried a semi-transparent thick plastic water bottle that he filled in the hallway leading through to the lamp-room. Now ready for action, Joe made his way with his mates to the bustling noisy lamp-room. He donned his lamp battery by sliding a thick leather brown belt through the lugs and then wrapped the belt around his waist and joined the large buckle. He swung the cable and lamp around his shoulder and let it dangle loosely on one side. He grabbed the two metal tallies from the hook adjacent to his lamp charger housing; one was brass in colour and the other silver grey, they both had the number 433 stamped on them, the same number as the lamp battery holder on the rack and on the lamp itself. The brass tally was handed to the banksman before entering the cage to go down the shaft and the silver grey one was left clipped to his belt and would be handed in to the banksman on returning to the surface. It was just one way of recording who was below ground and who was back on the surface.

The men trudged from the cage at the shaft bottom and walked forward in chattering groups along the underground galleries, splitting off here and there to different locations. Laughing, shouting, spitting, swearing and grumbling they continued into the mine towards the coal face locations and other work areas. They all knew where they were going and what lay ahead of them when they got there. Three-quarters of an hour later Joe and his mates had arrived at Piper 10's coal face, 150 yards below ground and two miles from the shaft down which they had been lowered.

'Here we go again,' said his collier mate Brian Smith as they took off their pullovers and shirts and bared themselves to their waists. Brian was Joe's brother-in-law, Mary's brother, he was a fantastic guy and extremely close to Mary.

'Too fucking right,' said Joe, 'what a way to make a bloody living – grovelling around like a bloody animal, shovelling your bollocks off for fifteen shillings a day. I should have been a butcher or done some other puffy job that would have kept me in the fresh air.'

'I can just see you as a butcher, Joey Murphy, swinging th'old sausage in front of all them ladies and giving the fellas a load of tripe.' Tom Booth always had a cynical retort.

'Bollocks, Tommy,' came the instant reply, 'you stand need to talk, five kids with two different women and three more you don't admit to.'

The men placed their sandwiches inside a small wooden box on the floor to keep them clear of the rats and mice. They tied their water bottles to the roadway supports to keep them slightly cooler in the ventilating air. They all took a relieving piss onto the mine floor because pissing on the coal face was often difficult and messy as they lay and worked in a three-quarter prone position. Another gulp of water and then the men went to their own respective tool rods to retrieve a shovel, pick and hammer. Seven other men were doing the same beside them in the return airway and ten others at the main intake roadway entrance to the coal face. The coal face required twenty colliers to work it, each with a ten-yard length of coal to blast and fill onto the flimsy belt conveyor. The coal face was barely three feet high and provided for a nightmare environment for the uninitiated.

It was a standard shift; the shotfirer blasted the coal, the colliers laboured in glistening black sweat, shovelling the coal onto the belt conveyor which stopped and started in underpowered irritation on a regular basis. Props and bars were set to support the roof and a mid-shift twenty minute break gave them time to eat their sandwiches, swill down water from their plastic water bottles, have another piss, a chat and a laugh. After their mid-shift break the colliers resumed their agonising work for a further two and half hours. The end of the shift couldn't come soon enough but it did eventually.

Ten men slid from under the coal face into the return

roadway. They were all as black as night. Coal dust, that had been on their sweaty, glistening bodies was now starting to dry out. Eyes were glistening red, dust coagulated to the corners of their eyelids, scratch marks were all over their muscular bodies, an occasional dribble of congealed blood was on their backs where they had caught the supporting bars as they manoeuvred one way and then another as they loaded the coal. Tools were locked onto tool rods for another shift, the last gulps of water were taken and shirts and pullovers were donned for the trek out of the mine.

The men snaked down the return roadway and trudged the two miles back to the shaft bottom. They were quieter now, initially tired to the point of exhaustion but still strong enough to recover now that the shovelling had finished. Walking was a doddle compared to the super-human efforts they had put in at the coal face. Soon half of them would be down on the allotment, winter digging ready for springtime. They reached the shaft bottom with a hundred other men and sat on the mine floor waiting for manriding to start at the shaft.

'For fuck's sake, start winding us up Billy, it's five past two. You've let those bastard deputies go up half an hour ago,' said one of the day-wage men to the onsetter.

'They went up at five to two and you'll go up at ten past two when I fucking let you,' said Billy. This was the only element of authority Billy Taylor had ever had in all his life and he clung onto it with fervour. He determined when the men would start manriding up the shaft and out of the mine – not them. In any event, if the men were too early onto the pit-top, he would get a good fucking from the

11

undermanager who was near to being God around these parts. Only the mine manager had greater authority than the undermanager and he *was* God. Ten past two came; the bells signalled for manriding. The men now stood up, inched themselves forward, twenty at a time onto the cage which, on the onsetter's final signal, eased gently upwards and then raced through the shaft, heading for daylight. All the dayshift men would be wound out of the pit in fifteen minutes, their grey tallies given to the banksman at the top of the shaft. Then they would continue on their journey back to the lamp-room, then the baths for a comforting and refreshing shower and then to their respective homes.

At 3.00pm exactly, Charlie Ross, the afternoon lamp-room attendant, started to check on dayshift lamps. He would make a note of any lamps that had not been returned to their racks for charging. Any gaps meant that some men were on overtime. Charlie made a list of numbers and names and compared it with the list that individual deputies had made out on their return to the surface. The dayshift men who were on overtime and still in the mine were recorded and cross-checked.

'Number 433, Joe Murphy, not yet back in,' mumbled Charlie. He checked against deputy Arthur Shelton's list of names of who would have been on overtime on Piper 10's. There were no names.

'That's funny, I wonder if Arthur has made a mistake.'

Charlie new that the deputies would be with the mine undermanager Geoff Dennis, reporting on the day's work, the problems, the requirements. He went over to the undermanager's office, knocked politely and opened the door.

'Sorry to bother you Mr. Dennis. Arthur, is Joey Murphy doing overtime, his lamp is not back in the rack?'

Geoff Dennis was a sophisticated man as far as undermanagers go. 'Charlie, have you received the tallies from the banksman yet?'

'No, boss.'

'Check with the banksman, I bet Joey has put his lamp in the wrong rack, he's probably halfway through his dinner by now.'

'OK, boss.'

Charlie went over to the lamproom and Bill Dodds, the banksman, was bringing his tin full of dayshift tallies for putting back on the lamp pegs.

'Hey up, Bill, seen Joey Murphy?'

'I think so – not sure.'

'Let's check the tallies, Bill.'

Charlie and Bill took handfuls of the tallies and returned them to the numbered pegs above the cap lamps in the racks, one at a time. The tin was empty; there was no number 433 tally.

'Bloody hell,' said Charlie, 'Arthur must have made a mistake, Joey Murphy must still be underground doin' summat. I'll go across to tell Arthur and Mr. Dennis.'

Charlie knocked on the door a second time. 'Sorry again Mr. Dennis, Arthur – Joey Murphy's tally is not back with the banskman, are you sure he's not on overtime?'

'Positive,' said Arthur Shelton, his voice barely disguising the first elements of concern.

The undermanager took control. 'Arthur, ring the afternoon deputy on Piper 10's, who is it?'

13

'John Hulme, boss.'

'That's right, give him a ring and ask him if anybody has seen Joey Murphy.'

Five minutes later a phone rang underground. 'Who's that?' said Arthur Shelton as a voice answered the primitive telephone in Piper 10's return gate.

'John Hulme.'

'John, Arthur here, where are you answering from?'

'From the return gate inbye end, Arthur, why?'

'Have you seen Joey Murphy on the way in John?'

'No.'

There was a butterflied intake of breath from the enquiring deputy. 'Fucking hell!'

'Why, what's up Arthur?'

'Joey's not back on the pit-top, John, where has he got to? Can you have the district searched please John, then give me a ring on pit-top? I'm not going home until I know Joey is safe, I'd better let Mr. Dennis know.'

'Mr. Dennis, we haven't traced Joey as yet, John's having the district searched and he's going to ring back. Shall we let his wife know?'

Undermanager Dennis hesitated thoughtfully for a moment – 'Let's give John time to have the district searched before we frighten Mrs. Murphy to death, Arthur. I know she's probably starting to worry a little but he's done overtime before and I'm sure she won't be panicking yet.'

Undermanager Dennis, overman Bill Thomas and deputy Arthur Shelton sat in the undermanager's office and sipped tea that had been made by Mr. Dennis' batman Ivan Johnson – it was now 3.45pm.

'Is there owt else you want before I make my way home, Mr. Dennis?'

'No thanks Ivan, be gone with you, have a good night – Jolly Colliers again is it? – see you tomorrow morning, don't get drunk.'

'Good day all.'

Ivan closed the door behind him. The three men shuffled on their chairs.

'I bet it's summat out of note,' said Bill Thomas, 'I'll brain that young bastard when I see him next.' He didn't mean it. All three would have given their right hands to know that nothing untoward had happened to Joe Murphy, although a good bollocking was on the cards irrespective.

'I'd better go and tell Mr. Chivers,' said the undermanager, a slight butterfly knot appearing in his abdomen.

Mine manager Peter Chivers was a bully of a man who stood way over six feet tall and weighed in at more than twenty stone. His red face permanently glistened with sweat and exuded a grimace of constant irritation in relation to everyone and everything around him. He exercised the power of his appointment with unrestrained vulgarity and had turned the belittling of those within earshot into an art form. Profanity and crudity were embodied genetically into his demeanour but he was capable of switching all of this off on the rare occasions he was in the presence of a senior. His reversion to an arse-licking demeanour was nothing short of a theatrical miracle, made even more embarrassing to those around him who suffered his vulgarity and wrath on a daily basis. His father had been group manager to the company's mines and he had followed in his father's footsteps but had never quite made the upper echelons of the company like his father. He remained at colliery manager level. That had made Peter Chivers bitter, and the best way of passing his bitterness on was to treat all about him like dirt. He did this with alacrity, in particular bossing his undermanager, and undermining him occasionally by giving instructions directly to the overmen without letting him know. He would criticise his undermanager for every single shortcoming that presented itself underground at the mine – lack of production, a roof fall, water ingress, a haulage rope failure, shortage of supplies – anything and everything. He swore continuously and thumped his desk like a demented animal, everyone at the mine was scared of him and averted their gaze when they saw him, or simply went the other way if they could.

Dennis knocked on the colliery manager's door and waited.

'Come in!' bellowed Chivers with a fearsome tone to his voice.

'Mr. Chivers, I thought I ought to let you know that we've got a little problem – we can't find Joe Murphy.'

'What do you mean, can't find Murphy, who the fuck is Murphy anyway?'

'A collier on Piper 10's, Mr. Chivers, lives on Bridge Street in Cotmanhay, has a wife and two kids.'

'Don't give me his fucking life history, what do you mean you can't find him? He can't have fucking disappeared.'

'His lamp is not back in the lamp-room and his tally has not been handed in,' said the undermanager.

'Has anybody been to his home?'

'Not yet.'

'Well there's your fucking answer then. The bastard will have gone home and forgotten to check out. He's probably stuck up his missus by now.'

'Joe is a responsible sort of bloke Mr. Chivers, he wouldn't take his lamp home by mistake and he's never been in trouble before, he's worked here for thirteen years and everyone respects him as a good collier.'

'Fuck him,' said the manager, 'the twat's in trouble this time, get somebody to his house pronto, and tell him I want to see him before he goes down this fucking pit again.'

CHAPTER TWO

The kitchen was simple but made to be functional. In the corner was a built-in copper boiler basin, stoked from a tiny cast-iron coal fire grate. Below that comprised a small rectangular built-in brick box, a base grid and a tiny cast-iron hinged door. There was a slot and a slide in the door to regulate the air flow and vary the burning speed of the coal fuel. The boiler provided hot water and the water would be ladled to the sink or the wash tub or the tin bath as and when required. Cold water was re-introduced to the boiler by the same ladle. The fire was made new every morning from old newspaper, a small amount of kindle wood and a few small coals. Ash was cleaned out from underneath every day with a small shovel and dumped in the ash bin outside. The walls of the kitchen were painted in pale yellowish gloss with varying grades of application.

There was a stone sink next to the boiler. It had one stark cold tap above it and a large rubber bung dangling on a chain to plug the drain hole. The kitchen floor had quarry-red tiles that still retained a meagre shine despite all the activity they had seen. In the far corner was a simple cooker which still boasted some of its green enamel sheen and a slightly cared for look. In the other corner, next to the entrance to the tiny living room, was a door to the stone pantry under the stairs. There was a wash tub near to the boiler and a metallic dolly with a strong wooden handle. In the middle of the quarry-tiled floor was a modest, wooden, rectangular table with a plastic table cover. There was the smell of a meat casserole in the oven and on the table were four metallic plates; two adult size and two for children. On the top of the cooker were two boiling pans with potatoes and cabbage. The kitchen was sparse, simple, warm and welcoming.

Mary Murphy was thirty-four years old and beautiful. She had a perfect figure, despite bearing two children, and she had deep black eyes and cheekbones to die for. She kept her dark brown hair short but with a brushed swirl that glistened with health and vigour. Her skin was slightly tanned, not from the sun but from a Spanish grandmother who she had never known. Genetically, she had been programmed to look distinctive and stunning. Her long brown woollen dress was simple but it didn't matter; such was her looks, style and deportment that she would have looked good in Cinderella rags.

Two boys were sitting on a pegged rug in front of a coal fire in the tiny, warm living room. There was a steel rod protective range around the tiled hearth to keep the children from harm. The boys were cutting out cardboard heart shapes with a pair of scissors; they were making flights for arrows. David was eleven and had his mother's dark features. Andrew was nine next month and was his father's double with fair hair, blue eyes and a square but kind jaw line. It was 4.35pm, there was a knock on the door.

Mary Murphy went to the door to see a middle-aged,

rather well-groomed man with a distinctive centre parting to his hair, a fresh complexion and dressed somewhat like a tailor. He was not the average neighbour. He had a slight air of authority but carried it with some reserve. There was a slight uncomfortable gaze to his demeanour.

'Mrs. Murphy?'

'Yes.'

'Wife of Mr. Joe Murphy?'

'Yes.' Panic had already set in to Mary Murphy's heart.

'I'm John Day, the mine training officer. Has Mr. Murphy returned home yet please?'

'No.' A silent heart-stopping pause. 'For God sake what's happened?'

'Don't worry – I'm sure there'll be a simple solution to all this. It looks as though Joe hasn't come out of the mine as yet but we've lost track of him for the moment. I'm sure he'll turn up. Actually he probably has come out of the mine and we've missed him. Gone to the pub or something and forgotten to leave his lamp behind.'

Mary Murphy looked at the training officer with irritation wrapped up in fear – 'My husband doesn't drink, Mr. Day.' It was said with some rare affirmation – not a quality that readily came to the fore with the collier's wife.

Panic had now turned to blind panic. What on earth was she to do? The cooker was on, the dinner was as good as done, the boys couldn't be left for any length of time in this situation. She didn't want to panic them either.

Mary covered her beautiful but now demented face with both hands. Her sublime world had turned to horror in a split second. Joe had undergone some dreadful accident, he was buried somewhere underground, nobody knew where, they'd never reach him, she would never see her wonderful husband again. She fainted.

Some minutes passed that Mary was unaware of and then: 'Mary, Mary, come on girl wake up.' It was Mrs. Taylor from next door. Mary opened her eyes slowly and gazed befuddled at the faces around her – Mrs. Taylor, her boys, Mrs. Joyce from across the road, and Mr. Day, still with the perfect parting but now with a concerned look of someone who had been the bearer of terrible news. She slowly raised herself into a seating position but, as she did so, her brain re-engaged with the bad news she had heard moments before. She screamed.

'Now, now, Mary, there's nothing for you to panic about yet. I remember all this happening to me when Mr. Taylor broke his leg at the pit and I got the message he had been rushed to hospital. Everybody thinks the worst, I'm sure there's a simple answer to all this.'

There may have been a simple answer but from Mary's perspective the world had just come to an end. She loved her husband beyond all measure, the boys adored him; life could not go on without him.

'I need to come to the mine,' she said.

'There's little or no point Mrs. Murphy,' said the training officer. His advice wasn't going to work; neither hell nor high water would prevent Mary Murphy from gathering her thoughts and going to the place where she was sure her husband would be. But what about the boys? Before she could even contemplate what to do with them, the answer came.

'If you're going to the mine Mary, I'll look after the boys.

Don't worry, I'll see to the cooker, their dinner, everything – you get yourself ready and get yourself gone.'

It wasn't the first time Mrs. Taylor had come to her rescue. *What is it about older people that they just know what to do and when to do it – and they do it gladly and for nothing?* Mary thought. She got to her feet, gathered herself, and went over to the cold tap above the sink. She doused her face lightly with a little cold water, smoothed her hair with her hands, took a deep breath, took her coat from the hook on the inside of the kitchen door and looked at the boys.

'Don't worry lads. Mummy needs to go to the pit. Mrs. Taylor will see to everything. I won't be long. If I am a little late, get your pyjamas on and get yourself to bed. Mrs. Taylor will keep an eye on you.' The words came out much braver than her bravery within.

She looked at Mr. Day who was obviously willing to give her his support despite the fact that his advice had not been heeded. He understood what Mary was going through and he was undoubtedly sympathetic. They set off together through the door and down the street, Mary almost invoking a scurry as though she thought that getting to the mine quicker would somehow rescue Joe sooner. Mr. Day led her to his relatively simple office and invited her to sit for a second. He went off down the corridor towards the mine manager's office. Within seconds, Mary could hear a booming voice in the corridor and shuffling feet.

'What on earth have you brought her here for Day, haven't we got enough on our fucking plate without dealing with some simpering bloody woman? We're down on coal output, costs are out of control, we have water breaking in down the

Low Main and a demented twat of a collier that's gone lost. What am I supposed to do with her? Get her to go home.'

'She's distraught Mr. Chivers, thinking the worst, it's understandable – ' He was cut off.

'Fuck distraught, I'm fucking distraught, having to deal with owners up my arse every fucking day, wanting to know what profit they're going to get come Friday. That's distraught, that's what being distraught is, that's fucking distraught mister.'

Mary had heard every word and was close to tears. Chivers and Day came round the corner to where she was sitting, forlorn, hopeless. She looked up at both men. Chivers cast his cruel red face and wicked eyes over Mary and was immediately taken aback by her beauty. He engaged into automatic arse-licking mode.

'Mrs. Murphy, I'm so sorry we seem to have this little problem with your Joe, don't worry, I'm sure he'll turn up before the night is out.'

'But where is he? This has never happened before,' Mary pleaded.

'Mr. Day, get Mr. Dennis here sharpish.'

The undermanager presented himself within two minutes.

'So what steps have you taken so far, Dennis, to find Mr. Murphy?'

'Mr. Chivers, I've contacted every deputy in the mine to check their districts thoroughly; they've all rung back, they haven't seen Joe.' Mary stumbled in part faint and Chivers responded like lightning.

'Now there there Mrs. Murphy, don't let's give up so

quickly. Let's go to the surveyors' office and review the situation over the mine plans. Day, Dennis, follow me – please come along Mrs. Murphy.' The group proceeded down the first corridor, then turned right along a second corridor before entering a large room with large tables. There were three men huddled over one of the tables looking at a giant plan spread out across it.

'You see Mrs. Murphy, this is a plan of the whole of the mine. Here, these two circles near to the middle of the plan are the mine shafts. One is used for winding coal and the other for winding men and materials in and out of the mine. Fresh air goes down one of the shafts and the polluted return air comes up the other. Why, there's a fan as big as your house that keeps this mine ventilated. And look here, this is where your husband works, Piper 10's district, two miles from the shafts and 150 yards below ground. I bet you never thought it was possible to get that far underground did you Mrs. Murphy?' Mary looked vacant; she could tell she was being patronised, she didn't want it – that was the last thing she wanted.

'And you see, your Joe would simply walk from the shafts to his coal face, shovel his coal and walk back again, it's that simple, isn't it Mr. Dennis?'

'It is, boss.'

'And all his mates would be with him, he can't get lost. There's no other way out of the mine – only through the shafts.'

There was a slight pause and then an intervention.

'Actually, Mr. Chivers, there is one other way.' It was the mine surveyor, Philip Smith.

'What's that Smith? Another way, what the bloody hell are you talking about?'

'I'm talking about Henshaw's Drift, Mr. Chivers. You know, the old return road that leads to the surface and serves as a second airway; the drift was originally part of Cossall mine next door. When Cossall closed, the drift, which had connected to our workings, was left open to serve as an emergency means of egress.'

'Of course I know about Henshaw's Drift, I'm the bloody mine manager aren't I? But it's never used, I only have it inspected once a month and the last report said that it was in a poor way and hardly travelable. We don't have to repair it by law because we have two means of egress to the mine via the shafts. Dennis, when was the last inspection made of Henshaw's Drift? Go and fetch me the report.'

The undermanager duly left with a nod of embarrassing obedience. Two minutes later he returned with a buff-coloured thick report book in his hand. On the front cover was writing in large blue ink capital letters: HENSHAW'S DRIFT.

'So when was it last inspected Dennis?' said Chivers.

Mr. Dennis peeled open the cover of the book and worked his way through the completed deputies' report sheets within. He got to the last completed page.

'It was last inspected about eight weeks ago, Mr. Chivers – December 5th 1937.'

'And which deputy signed the book, Mr. Dennis?'

'John Hulme.'

'And who was his accompanying workman?'

Mr. Dennis looked at the report. There was some

hesitation in his response. He raised his head slowly, his face turning white. There was a clear signature below the deputy's signature. 'The accompanying workman was… Joey Murphy, Mr. Chivers.'

Chivers contorted his mouth and clenched his teeth. He tried to partly constrain his utterance against all his natural inclinations – but without success.

'Fucking hell!' he murmured.

Chapter Three

The offices were plain but functional. All the doors except one were left open so that the occupants could be semi-aware of each other's existence and not feel imprisoned in any way. Two middle-aged men and another more elderly man sat in their respective offices at their respective modest desks. There were the obligatory "in", "pending" and "out" trays on each of the desks, each with papers and thick buff files, all at different levels in the trays and all marked with mine names and district names. In another office there was a rattle of typewriters and female voices exchanging dialogue, sometimes relating to work and sometimes to other things that females in an office setting like to pass the time of day with. The general environment was one of relaxed professionalism.

The office with the closed door was much larger than the others and it was fitted out with a larger, more shiny desk, a leather swivel chair, a deep blue functional carpet and, in one corner, a small conference table with six other standard chairs. In the swivel chair, smoking a pipe and exuding an air of quiet seniority, comfort and relaxation, sat Cyril Whatmore, His Majesty's Senior District Inspector of Mines and Quarries. To the side of Mr. Whatmore's office was a small secretarial office. The secretary's phone rang and Dawn Jones answered.

'Mr. Whatmore's office.' A pause. 'Yes he is in Mr. Chivers, I'll put you through.'

'It's Mr. Chivers, Oakwood Hills Colliery, Mr. Whatmore, he would like to speak to you directly.'

Cyril Whatmore was long in the tooth. As senior district inspector, he now visited mines very rarely, leaving the day to day work of inspections and enquiry to his district and, more particularly, his main grade inspectors who worked from home. But Whatmore had done the rounds. He'd been a main grade inspector for more than nine years and a district inspector for five years before gaining his appointment as senior district more than five years ago at the age of fifty-three. He knew the district like the back of his hand – and, more particularly, the people who managed the mines and quarries. He had seen Chivers' unprecedented rapid rise through the ranks from deputy to colliery manager despite his character flaws and bullying nature. The nepotism involved irked him. But Whatmore was too wise an owl to allow his view to cloud his greeting.

'Good morning, Mr. Chivers, how are you?' came the polite acknowledgement.

'I'm very well, thank you Mr. Whatmore, under constant pressure of course but managing to survive.'

'That's good. And how is Oakwood Hills colliery these days, I hear the Low Main seam is giving you some trouble?' Whatmore knew every coal seam in the district and all about the mining difficulties that presented themselves and the problems and accidents that arose.

'I'm afraid it's a pig of a seam, Mr. Whatmore,' said Chivers (he hated having to be condescending to any

28

inspector), 'a weak roof and a soft floor with some water ingress, can't hold the bloody roof up half the time but the men don't always help, you know what they're like sometimes, incapable of following instructions and adhering to my standards.'

The senior district inspector knew that whatever was wrong at Chivers' mine was somebody else's fault and that whatever was right at the mine was a direct result of Chivers' expertise and nobody else's. He had seen Chivers lie and scheme his way to seniority all his career and he had witnessed his father get him out of a hole on more than one occasion on his rapid rise to fame.

'What is it that I can do for you, Mr. Chivers?' said the inspector, drawing on his pipe and waiting for the manager to respond.

'We've had rather a peculiar situation at the mine this past twenty-six hours or so Mr. Whatmore, nothing for you to get involved with but I thought I would notify you out of courtesy – you know I like to keep you informed.'

Whatmore knew that Chivers was one of those colliery managers who would be the last to let an inspector know anything out of courtesy. His natural tendency was to hide everything he could both from the inspectorate and from his senior managers. As the mine manager, he was captain of his own little ship and everybody else knew three-quarters of fuck all. Chivers had a niggling situation he couldn't avoid and he knew that if he didn't let the inspector know, the jungle drums would.

'Precisely what is it you have to tell me, Mr. Chivers?' said Whatmore in an unruffled, guardedly controlled voice.

'At the present moment in time,' said Chivers, 'we appear to have lost a collier. He went underground at the normal time yesterday on the seven o'clock day shift but didn't report back to the lamp-room at the end of the shift. He wasn't doing overtime and we've had the mine searched from top to bottom and we can't find him. We think he's probably done a runner with some tart, you know what these men are like, no moral standing. In any event, nothing for you to bother with Mr. Whatmore, I'll keep you informed of developments. He's probably buggered off to Skegness, likely to be home before the week is out.'

Whatmore drew back on his pipe. The colliery manager's persuasive mode didn't have any effect. 'Most peculiar, Mr. Chivers; not come across this one before. And you say you've had the mine searched from top to bottom?'

'All the active places, Mr. Whatmore, every deputy's district, all the main roads, the shaft bottoms, salvage districts and development districts. We've checked every pump lodge, every engine room and all the underground offices and stores.'

'What about the old abandoned districts, Mr. Chivers? I recognise it's not easy, what with the possibility of blackdamp and what have you – how have you gone about that?'

'We've had good discipline in recent years in sealing off the old abandoned workings while I've been manager here, Mr. Whatmore. The very old abandoned workings that previous managers didn't seal off have now collapsed and access is impossible as far as I know. Leave it with me and I'll keep you informed.'

'That's very kind of you, Mr. Chivers. In the meantime,

I'll send Mr. Wrigley to have a little chat with you – you know, to see if there's anything we can do to help.'

'That's very kind of you, Mr. Whatmore,' said the manager, now gritting his teeth, 'when will Mr. Wrigley be coming, tomorrow?'

'No, I'll send him directly.'

'OK Mr. Whatmore, thank you very much, have a good afternoon.'

'And a very good afternoon to you, Mr. Chivers.'

Chivers waited for the click at the other end of the line and then slammed his phone down like a demented gorilla.

'Interfering bastard!' he bellowed.

CHAPTER FOUR

The black shiny Ford saloon pulled into the colliery pit yard and toddled its way slowly to the car parking space next to the colliery manager's, which was marked with a small wooden sign, "Reserved for HMI". District inspector Ken Wrigley applied the handbrake but even before he could open the car door, Ivan Johnson appeared directly to the driver's side.

'Good morning Mr. Wrigley, can I carry anything for you? Will you be going underground, are your pit clothes in the boot sir?'

'Good morning Ivan, that's very kind of you but I think I need to speak to Mr. Chivers first before I decide whether there's a need to go underground or not. Anyway, how are you keeping?'

'I'm very well Mr. Wrigley, all things considered, that Guinness keeps me in good fettle and generally out of trouble, except for the wife of course. Please follow me Mr. Wrigley and let me carry your briefcase.'

Johnson led Wrigley down the well-trodden path to the manager's office. He knocked on the door and opened it. 'Mr. Wrigley to see you Mr. Chivers, he doesn't know if he is going underground as yet Mr. Chivers, so I have left Mr. Wrigley's pit clothes in his boot, please give me a shout if you will be wanting them Mr. Wrigley.'

Wrigley knew that Johnson was exercising the standard protocol whenever one of HM inspectors visited the mine. Was he going underground and where was he going to? As soon as they knew, the surface telephone attendant would be alerted and he would be immediately on the phone to the relevant deputy below ground. Whatever could be put right in the deputy's district before the inspector actually got there might save some embarrassment all round.

Chivers stood almost to attention and the two men shook hands. In the mining industry, an HM Inspector of Mines was treated with great care and attention. The inspector had the power to "stop the job", or direct that improvements were made, or to ask and make enquiry of anyone about anything concerning safety at work and, in the last analysis, to prosecute companies and individuals, including colliery managers. In the main they had great respect and were recognised to be on everybody's side and particularly that of the workmen if their health and safety was at risk and procedures were not being followed. HM Inspectors were responsible for the enforcement of the complex health and safety law as it applied to mines and quarries. All inspectors had been trained in the mines and had been in positions of seniority before taking up their governmental civil service posts. Ken Wrigley was extremely well respected; even Peter Chivers was aware that he wasn't a man that could be hoodwinked or one who could be bribed or corrupted in some fashion that would lead to an advantage. Any colliery manager who might try to undermine Wrigley in any way would be on dangerous ground.

'So,' said Wrigley, 'you've apparently made history, Mr. Chivers – lost a collier somewhere or other, tell me about it.'

Chivers gave all the details he could to the inspector. He was convinced that somewhere along the line there was a simple explanation and Murphy would turn up and the episode would come to a close as quickly as it had started.

'You know what some of these colliers are like, Mr. Wrigley. They think everything is a bloody joke sometimes, I'll kill the bugger myself when he turns up.'

'You said that you've had the whole of the underground searched, Mr. Chivers?'

'Everywhere.'

'And have you notified the police? We have a missing person on our hands, have we not?'

Chivers raised his eyebrows, trying to hide a degree of frustration. 'Didn't think it was a police matter, Mr. Wrigley. After all I didn't want to get them into some wild goose chase, all that time and expense and what have you.'

'I think you should notify them. The man has been missing for more than twenty-six hours now, nobody knows where he is, I'm sure his family are distraught and we don't know if he has been in an accident or if there is some other explanation to his disappearance.' The inspector was quietly adamant as to what should be done.

'I'll notify them directly, Mr. Wrigley.' The colliery manager grudgingly picked up his phone and gave all the details to the local police station at Ilkeston. The inspector listened to the message and the matter-of-fact tone of the colliery manager. There was no doubt that there would be a visit from the local constabulary shortly. The colliery manager knew he would now have a double whammy; the local police and the local mines inspector on his premises – and his irritating expression conveyed itself to the inspector – *and all for fuck all* – he was thinking.

'Before the police get here, Mr. Chivers, remind me of the mine layout and of the means of egress from the mine, two shafts and an old drift if I remember correctly.' The inspector knew the layout of the mine almost as well as the manager, better in some regards; he had been an inspector in the district for more than ten years.

'If you are as certain as you can be that Murphy didn't leave the mine via the shafts then he must either still be underground or has got out of the mine via Henshaw's Drift. You say you have had Henshaw's Drift examined?'

'From one end to the other, Mr. Wrigley.'

'And by the way, the law requires you to inspect all airways at least once a month, Mr. Chivers,' said the inspector, partly admonishingly. 'How come you've left it nearly eight weeks?'

'Nobody uses the drift Mr. Wrigley, it doesn't seem a very productive exercise to spend manshifts inspecting an airway which is only there in an emergency.'

'The law has a purpose, Mr. Chivers, the roadway might be needed in an emergency at any time, the very reason you have kept it open. What is the point of having an emergency means of egress if you don't check its condition at the proper statutory intervals to ensure that it is suitable for purpose?' The manager didn't reply.

'And what else can you tell me about the condition of the drift, Mr. Chivers, what did the deputy have to say? And let me have sight of his report please.' Chivers picked up his phone and dialled. 'Mr. Dennis, bring the report book for Henshaw's Drift to my office straight away.'

The undermanager arrived with the report book almost immediately.

'Please remain here Mr. Dennis,' said the inspector, 'and how are you keeping? Somewhat of an unusual set of circumstances this disappearance, Mr. Dennis?'

'It is Mr. Wrigley,' replied the undermanager. He had one eye on Chivers who he recognised to be inwardly incensed that the inspector had invited him to remain in the manager's office. Only Chivers dealt with the bigwigs at this mine; everyone else ran about to serve his every request. The manager enjoyed demonstrating his extreme authority over all those about him, especially to inspectors. Wrigley was conscious of the atmosphere about him and quietly revelled in the fact that he had overarching authority, if not direct executive command. His authority extended to asking any persons at the mine to assist him with his enquiries and that included asking Mr. Dennis to remain in the manager's office and to answer any questions he put to him. He knew Dennis to be a good and candid man and someone who would endeavour to help all he could, despite the proximity of the tyrant in the room.

'Tell me Mr. Dennis,' said the inspector, opening the deputy's report book for Henshaw's Drift at the same time, 'who was the deputy that made the inspection of the drift late yesterday and what did he have to say?'

'It was Brian Ramsbottom,' interjected the colliery manager, 'and he found little or note that is of relevance, Mr. Wrigley, his report doesn't read up to much, does it Mr.

Dennis?' The colliery manager had obviously not read the report in any detail. He was obviously dismissive of Henshaw's Drift being of any significance.

The undermanager gathered himself to inform the inspector what the deputy had found on his inspection of Henshaw's Drift. He knew and could feel that this was going to incense Chivers but he also knew that it was his duty to inform the inspector of the details even if it meant taking the rap from the mine manager afterwards. Being economical with the truth was a particular expertise of the manager's that the undermanager had not yet acquired.

The undermanager related that Henshaw's Drift was some 400 yards long and inclined from the workings to the surface at a very steep gradient of about 1 in 3. The deputy's report referred to the condition of the drift in some detail. It was supported by steel arches some ten feet wide by eight feet high and the arches were lagged with wooden boards. The report described some normal deformation of the arches not unusual in coal mines, particularly in a drift of this age which had been partially affected by coal workings in close proximity. Many of the lagging boards had rotted over the years and numerous ones had split or even broken, allowing the overlying broken shales and mudstones to dribble out and fall to the floor. Again, this was not unusual and such minor falls did not necessarily affect the overall integrity of the drift or make it untravellable for the purposes of emergency egress. Over the years, some of the more significant falls had been repaired with new lagging boards but much of the debris that had fallen out had either been left in situ, because it wasn't much, or had been levelled out to make a passable walking track. Repairing the drift over the years meant that new boards had to be carried to site by the repair men because it had not been possible, or thought necessary, to maintain a rail track for normal pony transportation purposes. The report referred to "two recent falls", one only some thirty yards into the drift from its lowest point and another fall, "about 150 yards from the surface". The lower fall was described as "fresh", the deputy probably having noted the lack of dust and oxidation on the newly fallen debris. It was some five yards long and about two feet deep. The fall only 150 yards from the surface was described as "relatively fresh", some eight yards long and about three feet deep. The deputy had suggested that they were "both in need of some light repair and lagging". The drift was reported as being "satisfactorily ventilated" with "no significant methane present". The drift was "travelable with care" but in "need of some repair".

'Hmm!' said Wrigley thoughtfully, 'I think it's worth investigating these two new falls a little more closely Mr. Chivers, what do you think?'

'I really can't see much point,' replied the manager, but he was conscious that he wasn't going to win the argument. The request from the inspector would resort to an instruction backed up by a formal "notice" if push came to shove. The manager capitulated and hid his annoyance by a pretence of wanting to appear more than helpful.

'OK, if you think this is worthwhile Mr. Wrigley.' He looked at undermanager Dennis and, with an instruction camouflaging his resignation, said in a forthright tone, 'Get a collier to either end of both falls as soon as you can, like now, and let them dig through the falls and see what they come up with.'

'Right boss,' said the undermanager, preparing to leave the room, 'I'll get that sorted immediately. I'll keep you informed Mr. Wrigley.'

'How long will it take you to get the colliers to site, Mr. Dennis?' enquired Mr. Wrigley.

'About an hour.'

'And to clean through the falls?'

'About two hours.'

'Sounds about right to me. I'll tell you what,' replied the inspector, 'I'll stay on the pit-top until I hear from below ground; it will give me an opportunity to speak to the police with Mr. Chivers.' The manager's face remained passively blank.

The inspector and mine manager remained in the mine office and, within two minutes of the undermanger leaving, Ivan Johnson knocked and entered, bringing in a pot of tea and two heavy mugs on a tray with milk and sugar. The inspector offered his thanks to Ivan and the manager ignored him. As the manager poured the tea, there was another knock on the door.

'Mr. Chivers,' said Ivan Johnson, 'It's Sergeant Pollard of the Ilkeston Police.'

Sergeant Pollard entered the manager's office in a polite and respectful manner but with an authority that had been honed over twenty-five years of service.

'Gentlemen?'

'Good afternoon Sergeant,' said Chivers. 'I'm Peter Chivers, mine manager, and this is Mr. Wrigley, HM District Inspector of Mines and Quarries.' The men shook hands.

'We're sorry to bother you Sergeant, but we have a bit of

a problem at the mine and we thought you should know,' said Chivers. 'Mr. Wrigley considered it only courteous to keep you in the picture. For my own part, I think we might be on a fool's errand and I'm worried we might be wasting your time.'

'I've got all the time in the world Mr. Chivers. What's the problem?'

The problem was explained to the police sergeant in some detail. He made notes. He asked only a few questions and it was clear that his powers of rationalisation were astute. He had already recognised that Mr. Wrigley was his main link to taking matters forward.

'So what do you suggest, gentlemen? Underground is your expertise and, Mr. Wrigley, you have primary enforcement authority on this site – until of course somebody tells me there has been a criminal misdemeanour.'

Before the manager could respond, Wrigley quickly interjected.

'I agree with you Sergeant; make the enquiries you have spoken about, go along to see Mrs Murphy as you have suggested, we'll deal with the mine situation and we will let you know immediately if we find something untoward.'

'Sounds good to me, gentlemen, this is a new one on me but I'm sure it won't be long before we get to the bottom of it. I wish you good day.' The men shook hands and the sergeant left the office to be met by Ivan Johnson who escorted him to a waiting police car.

'Let's have a walk to the surveyors' office, Mr. Chivers. I need to look a little closer at the mine plan and mull a few things over.'

'Fair enough Mr. Wrigley. In the meantime I'll order you some lunch.'

After lunch, the inspector asked for a private office and made a few phone calls.

Subsequently, there was a knock on the door; it was Peter Chivers with a sheepish white look on his face. 'Mr. Wrigley,' he paused for an added intake of breath, 'Mr. Dennis has been on the phone – they've found Joey Murphy – under the rock fall near to the bottom of Henshaw's Drift – he's dead.'

The inspector stroked his chin slowly. 'Tell them not to move Mr. Murphy's body. Send a message to Sergeant Pollard and ask if he will be coming back to the mine or if he will be sending the coroner's officer in his stead.' He paused. 'And ask Ivan Johnson to get my pit clothes from the back of my car and bring them to your bathroom, Mr. Chivers, please; I'm going underground.'

CHAPTER FIVE

The beautiful, dark-haired woman lifted the china teapot and poured tea into a china cup sitting on a "country roses" saucer. She glanced through her kitchen window at a small, tidy garden and across the low privet hedge at the bottom onto a field where sheep were grazing. The day was cold but there was a clear blue sky and the early morning frost had just about lifted.

The kitchen was small but exquisite. There was a solid fuel boiler in one corner, a gleaming gas cooker opposite, a white porcelain sink with hot and cold running taps and a small cottage-type settee with a woollen blanket strewn neatly over it. The solid fuel boiler kept the kitchen warm and homely and a central rug added to the cosiness of the room. There were early daffodil bulbs just pushing through in a vase on the windowsill.

Lily Daykin was thirty-six and a divorcee. Being a divorcee and living on your own in this locality was a rarity. She had no children.

The house was semi-detached but no bigger than a two-up, two-down terrace. There were only twelve houses in total in the hamlet of Strelley Grange together with a pub – the Black Swan – and, about a half mile away, a farmhouse owned by William Jones. The concrete lane leading to the hamlet was only single track in most places and it had high hawthorn hedgerows and a drainage ditch running on either side. Over the hedgerows were fields that yielded fine arable crops every year without fail. The fields were stark at this time of the year but come July they would have a bountiful magnificence and beauty of their own – England in its prime and country best.

Lily glanced pensively through the window. She was waiting for scones to complete their cooking in the oven and she was taking in their smell and aroma quietly and rewardingly. Living on her own had not stopped her doing all her own cooking and baking and, in this locality, vegetables were cheap and readily available. Only meat from the butcher's shop in the main Strelley village was moderately expensive. Her income was modest but sufficient. A seamstress by training, she made and modified clothes in her own front room using an electric sewing machine. She had an exceptional gift for invoking some degree of style and quality into her work, which pleased many of her customers in the village and hamlet. Her own clothes also exuded style, irrespective of the absolute quality of the materials used, although she was usually able to recognise and buy quality for a fair price, particularly in Nottingham. She supplemented her income with a cleaning job at the Black Swan on Saturday and, sometimes, Sunday mornings.

Looking beyond the sheep in the field, Lily could see the arched entrance/outlet of Henshaw's Drift which was not more than one hundred yards away from her rear garden. The outlet was unobtrusive, even in this country setting. An entrance arch and an angled continuum disappeared at a sharp gradient into the ground. There was a light mesh fence to stop persons entering the mine but which could be lifted easily and swung open by those exiting the drift on the rare occasions that they did so. Near to the entrance, the ground was worn of grass and there was a light muddy patch which rapidly turned to natural grass cover within a few strides. On very quiet days she could hear the slight drone of a ventilating fan which must have been positioned well into the drift to avoid causing a nuisance to the people living in the hamlet.

There were some quiet but complicated thoughts in her mind as she gazed towards the outlet of Henshaw's Drift. She had seen miners in their blackened frames, usually in pairs, exit the mine from time to time over the years. She was in awe that human beings could work in such dark, god-forsaken places while she had spent the whole of her life in the fresh air being able to watch the seasons change and the beauty of the countryside. On occasions she had been in the back garden and acknowledged the men as they trudged past in their pit gear. She had offered them a mug of tea on occasions in winter and a cool drink of barley water in summer.

As her stare glazed over, there was a large earnest knock at the front door. She startled back into conscious mode and walked smartly through the stylish front room – she opened the door – it was Mrs. Lacey from next door.

'Lily, have you heard the bad news? The postman's just told me – he's just come from delivering mail to the mine, there's been a fatal accident, they're saying one of the colliers has been killed with a roof fall – a young fella, somebody called Murphy – Joey Murphy – apparently the poor lad's got a wife and two small kids, they live in Cotmanhay.'

Lily Daykin stood motionless and her face drained of blood in an instant. She collapsed like a sack of potatoes.

CHAPTER SIX

The inspection party set off underground. Peter Chivers to the fore, followed by HM District Inspector Wrigley, undermanager Dennis, the mine safety officer Bill Price, two union men and a workmen's inspector who represented the men and was an employee at the mine. Dr. Parson, who was on call to the mine, had gone into the mine just before them together with the mine medical attendant and a nurse.

The party snaked quietly through the mine galleries and after about three-quarters of an hour reached a right-hand turn about 150 yards away from Piper 10's return roadway entrance. This short cross-cut led to the bottom of Henshaw's Drift. At the bottom of the drift was a mine telephone and a day-wage man was positioned there in case there were any incoming calls trying to make contact with the rescue people at the accident site. Looking up the drift, the party could see a group of cap lamps about twenty yards away. The lamps were mainly still and the party found the rescue group in a quiet sombre mood, resting and waiting for the inspector and colliery manager.

Overman Harris greeted the party. 'Sad day Mr. Chivers, there's Joey.' He gestured to the floor of the roadway where Joey Murphy's body lay pitifully, splayed out flat to the floor

46

with his arms stretched forward above his head. The colliers had cleaned much of the debris away from the body by a process of rembling – throwing it back to each other in turn, both up and down the drift, as they knelt on the mine floor. A number of the men at the site had tears or dried tears and were obviously but quietly distraught. Joey's helmet and camp lamp were trailed backwards towards his feet with the cap lamp battery still held at his waste by the strong leather belt.

Dr. Parson had officially confirmed his death. 'It looks as though the poor man has been suffocated,' he said. 'This blue colour to the side of his face and to his hands signifies that rocks may have crushed his chest cavity and prevented him from breathing. At first glance, I cannot see major effects of trauma, although I haven't moved the body as you requested.'

Chivers noted that a stretcher had already been brought to site by the rescue team. 'Right,' he said, 'load Joey onto the stretcher gently lads, let's get him covered up and out of the mine.'

'Wait for a moment,' said Wrigley – there was a long pause. 'I'm really very sorry to ask this but could everyone here please leave the site for just a couple of minutes – except of course you, Mr. Chivers, Mr. Dennis, Dr. Parson, Sergeant Pollard and one of the workmen's inspectors.' The others present looked surprised but their faces acknowledged that the mines inspector was in charge and would have good reason to put in his request. The rest grouped together and walked disconsolately to the bottom of the drift and sat in the short cross-cut road, resting and talking plaintively.

'What's going through your mind, Inspector?' asked

Chivers with a slight hint of irritation. 'It looks straightforward to me. The poor bugger's probably come in here to relieve himself or something and by rotten coincidence, the roof has decided to slip out and trap him. Maybe it was simply the vibration he was causing or perhaps he has accidently snagged a board and caused a flush of stone to fall out.'

'Mr. Chivers, I'm not so sure,' said Wrigley with a quiet authority. 'Sergeant Pollard, would you in particular be kind enough to take a note of my observations?'

The inspector continued. 'Firstly, take a look at the body and its immediate proximity to the ground. Joey's body is fully stretched out, arms straight above his head pointing towards the top of the drift and his legs nearly straight as a dye. If he was standing up when the roof fall occurred, I would have expected some of the debris to have been under his body as it fell out and pushed him to the floor from his vertical position. In any event, in a roof fall of this nature, I wouldn't have expected Joey to be stretched out as he is, but bent or contorted in some way or other.'

'You know Mr. Wrigley,' said undermanger Dennis, 'I think you've got something there.' The inspector could see Chivers starting to squirm with irritation. The manager didn't want a straightforward roof fall developing into a clever-dick manipulation of something it wasn't by an interfering twat of an inspector.

Wrigley cupped his fingers around his chin and partly over his mouth. There was something not right in what he was observing. He looked at the debris on the floor that had been shovelled up and down the drift, off and away from Murphy's body. There were occasional old broken lagging board pieces amongst the shale and mudstones. He noticed two pieces on the upper side of the body and three on the lower that had fresh pick indentation marks. He looked round and could see only miners' round-nosed shovels in the vicinity; there were no picks at the site. He glanced at the roof above the body where the shales and mudstones had flushed out and covered Joey Murphy. To the edges of the roof fall, in that part of the roof that still remained intact, where the old lagging boards remained in situ, albeit some hanging down, he could see occasional fresh pick marks on the boards and a scraping of pick indentations in the mudstone at the fringes in the mine roof.

'Sergeant Pollard,' said Wrigley with quiet authority, 'I think we should declare this a crime scene. You'd better get your forensic experts here quickly; there's much to do. Mr. Chivers, please ask just one of your deputies to stand guard at the telephone point at the bottom of the drift; the rest can go. I suggest you don't work Piper 10's district for the time being. I'm very sorry about all this but we need to be absolutely clear on what has happened here.'

'If that's what you want,' retorted Chivers with resigned frostiness. 'God knows what this is going to cost us. Mr Dennis, get things organised and let's be sharp about it. If we lose coal on Piper 10's for too long, we're all going to get the fucking push.'

CHAPTER SEVEN

'I've conducted the post-mortem Sergeant Pollard,' said Dr. Phillipa West, 'and you were right,' she continued on the phone. 'I presume you will want to take photographs of the body?'

'Yes, Doctor, I'll have our photographer come over straight away, I'll come with him – should be there within the hour.'

The police sergeant and the photographer were greeted at the hospital reception and taken through to the autopsy unit by a young nurse. Dr. West was standing at a counter, filling in notes as they arrived; she put down her pen and greeted the two police representatives solemnly with a shake of the hand. 'Follow me,' she said as she led them through a double door into a cold room with a stark stone-block table in the middle. She peeled back a cotton sheet to expose Joey Murphy's body. The collier's body was rigid but paradoxically it exuded beautiful maleness. Joey was lithe and muscular, his body formed and moulded by more than ten years of mind-numbing hard work, shovelling coal on a coal face no more than three feet high. A body that had twisted, turned, sweated, glistened and driven itself almost beyond recognisable human stamina for five days a week, year in year out. This was a physique wholly in its prime, now utterly and completely lifeless. From the waist upwards, Joey was blackened with coal dust. The dust was pasted into dried-out sweat that had once been steaming hot but which was now clammy and cold. His hair was frizzled and riddled with dust and his face was contorted with the last throes of unimaginable pain. Below the waist he was relatively clean, protected by his thick pit trousers as he had knelt and worked. This was a man who had been in his physical prime, now captured for eternity by a single act of aggression.

'Look closely here, sergeant.' Dr. West pointed to Murphy's lower front neck. There were two brutal indents. 'The poor man has been strangled. These indents have been made by thumbs throttling with intense might, so much so that you can see the brownness of blood at the bottom of each indentation. Now that I have cleaned the back and sides of the neck, you can see where the killer's fingers have gripped tightly so as to enable the thumbs to dig into his throat.'

The policeman gazed at the pitiful sight before him and felt a tear come to his eyes. He had seen death many times before but the collier looked hopeless and tragic, dirty yet beautifully defined, blackened and lifeless. 'May I use your phone Doctor?'

The doctor nodded, 'Certainly, please do.'

'It's Sergeant Pollard here Mr. Wrigley, your suspicions were well founded, Joey Murphy has been strangled, we've got a murder on our hands.'

CHAPTER EIGHT

There was a knock on the door. It was opened slowly and Sergeant Pollard was greeted by a senior to middle-aged man in a disconsolate tone. 'Yes?'

'I'm Sergeant Pollard of the Ilkeston Police sir and this is Constable Emma Blake. Is Mrs. Mary Murphy in please?'

'Yes, my daughter is in, please come inside Sergeant.'

There were five or six people in the small living room but the atmosphere was one of dejection and disbelief. In the corner, Mary Murphy was sitting in a small armchair. Her still beautiful face now had deeply reddened eyes and she stared with a mild demented gaze at the coal fire that glittered to her right. To her left, kneeling and looking at her with distress, was her mother Margaret Smith. She was cupping Mary's hand in both of hers, trying her hardest to induce any fragment of comfort she could.

'Come on sweetheart, I know it's hard, but try to be brave, you need to be for the boys' sake, they'll be home from school in a couple of hours.'

'I can't, Mother. He was my life, he was the boys' best friend, he was our breadwinner, our rock. How can we possibly go on? Who is going to look after us? How are we going to pay the bills? Who is going to teach the boys all the things that boys should know and do? This is unbearable.' Mary cupped her face into her hands and started to sob quietly. Sergeant Pollard averted his gaze and Emma Blake looked at the floor with innate sadness. The mother caressed her daughter even closer. There was silence.

'I'd better make a cup of tea,' said Terry Smith. 'Sergeant, Constable, how do you take it? Everybody else want a cuppa?' Mr. Smith retreated to the kitchen followed by his other daughter Tess. Doing something at this juncture, anything, prevented the pain and distress from exploding. Five minutes later tea was served.

'Mrs. Murphy,' said Pollard, 'there is something very painful I need to tell you and I'm wondering if you had best be on your own?'

'Painful, what do you mean painful?' said the widow. 'How can anything be more painful than what has already happened? Do you know what it is like to lose your most precious friend, Sergeant, have you ever been in this position?' And then with a voice from a broken heart, 'I cannot begin to describe the pain!'

It was an unfair question but the sergeant took it on the chin. He took a deep breath.

'I can't imagine what it must be like Mrs. Murphy, I just can't.' A pause. 'But there is something it is my duty to tell you and you may wish to be in private.'

Mary Murphy looked around the room at all the faces that she loved, desperate and confused. The faces reciprocated their pity. She gathered herself bravely.

'There's no need for privacy here, Sergeant, this is my mother and father, my brother Brian, my sister Tess and

Joey's sister Rachael – these are my closest family, we have no secrets here, please say what you have to say.'

'Are you sure?'

Almost indignantly: 'Yes, I'm sure.'

The sergeant hesitated and took in another large deep breath. 'Mrs. Murphy, I am afraid to say we do not now believe that your husband died of a simple accident.' Mary looked up incredulously; she was utterly perplexed. 'What on earth do you mean?'

Before the sergeant could respond, Brian Smith dived in with interjection. 'Don't be silly Sergeant, I work with the bloke, he's like a brother to me, he was buried under a fall of ground, of course it was a bloody accident.'

'I'm afraid it wasn't, Mr. Smith.' The sergeant raised his tone slightly, more formally, 'We have strong evidence to suggest that he was murdered, strangled to death.' Mary Murphy gave out a piercing scream; this was all too much.

CHAPTER NINE

The men sat around a large oak table in the mine conference room and cigarette smoke pervaded the atmosphere. There was a large mug of tea in front of all of them that Ivan Johnson had served with a degree of quiet humility. Chivers, the mine manager, sat at the head of the table, flanked by Mines Inspector Wrigley and Police Sergeant Pollard. Next to Pollard was a small man with a black pencil moustache and a balding head. Also seated were undermanager Dennis, safety officer Bill Price, mine surveyor Philip Smith, training officer John Day, the trade union secretary Albert Mater and a workmen's inspector Barry Hogarth.

'Mr. Chivers,' said Sergeant Pollard, 'perhaps I should start by introducing Detective Inspector Brian Maddox to you. Mr. Maddox is from the Derby CID.' The bald man with the pencil moustache glanced at everyone round the table and dipped his head modestly.

'Thank you Mr. Wrigley,' responded Chivers. In turn he introduced every one of the mine staff seated around the table to the detective inspector. Then with a show of semi-disguised bravado, 'How would you like to play this Mr. Maddox? I've already lost a day's production on Piper 10's, the pit can't stand it, if we don't make 5,000 tons this week

I'm going to have my knackers snatched and there's going to be some serious questions asked by the owner.'

The detective looked forward slowly, he put the thumbs of both hands beneath his chin with his elbows resting on the edge of the large table, he lowered his eyes slightly and signalled a demeanour to all present of being completely unphased by the manager's remarks. He let a few seconds of silence elapse.

'It would seem to me, Mr. Chivers, that you have a more serious problem on your hands than this week's production,' responded Maddox with a quiet but steely authority. 'A wife has lost her husband, two children their father and a murderer operates on your premises and none of you know who he is or what his motives might be. Perhaps he has another victim in mind, perhaps he is a psychopath and all your employees are in potential danger.' He took a direct look with penetrating eyes at the colliery manager. 'For the removal of any doubt, Mr. Chivers, this mine is under criminal investigation and I expect co-operation from everybody on these premises no matter what their seniority.'

The colliery manager squirmed slightly in his chair but tried to avoid giving off any other signal of discomfort or embarrassment. He was the one around this place who issued the uncontrolled, vulgar, sickening orders – and bollockings – and he didn't take kindly to there being other people or authorities present who might overrule or dictate to him. It was enough with a fucking mines inspector being on site, let alone a police inspector. His efforts to hide his discomfort didn't work but the underlings around the table avoided giving out any signals that would indicate that "it served the bastard right".

'Oh! Please don't get me wrong Inspector,' responded Chivers with a slight air of awkward patronisation. 'You'll be getting all the help you want from us, won't he Mr. Dennis?' To ask the undermanager for back-up was akin to swallowing horse muck. The undermanager nodded affirmatively but far more out of respect for the detective than his mine manager, although he wasn't going to give the game away.

'Just tell us what arrangements you want putting into place Inspector Maddox and we'll action them immediately.' The undermanager looked the policeman directly in the eye. The mine manager was inwardly livid that his pathetic undermanager was already gaining more respect than he would ever be able to.

The detective inspector had investigated his fair share of murders but never before underground at a coal mine. Under the normal scheme of things, the mines inspectorate were the government's statutory enforcing authority for underground coal mine matters. They would investigate serious coal mine accidents, including fatalities, and the police would just offer support via the coroner's officer. The mines inspectorate had good relations with coroners generally and would provide all the evidence he would need for any inquest, including copies of witnesses' statements that they had taken during their investigations. It was impossible for a police inspector to readily appreciate the operations and protocols operating at a mine and this was going to be an exceptionally difficult challenge for Maddox. Mines inspector Wrigley was aware of the dilemmas that might present themselves to the police inspector and new intuitively that he needed to lend support.

'Perhaps I could come in here Inspector Maddox?' said

Wrigley, catching the detective's eye and signalling his support by nothing more than a professional glance. Maddox was wise enough to recognise the signal of help being offered by the mines inspector.

'Thank you very much,' said the police inspector, 'how do you think we should proceed, Mr. Wrigley?'

The mines inspector had already figured out how best the enquiry could proceed in his own mind and had formulated a list of bullet points that represented an action programme. 'Your police forensic team have already been to the direct location where Mr. Murphy's body was found and have looked around the general area. Can I suggest that I get my team of mines inspectors in and we examine the whole of Piper 10's district, the route into the district from the shafts, the cross-cut leading to Henshaw's Drift and the drift itself right through to the surface at Strelley Grange? We can also interview witnesses from the dayshift, afternoon shift and night shift and determine Joey Murphy's shift pattern and his final movements. I'm sure you would like to have some of your police officers present when we conduct our physical inspections and interview crucial witnesses, Inspector Maddox?'

Maddox was quietly grateful for the structured response from the mines inspector. 'Your proposals seem to have a great deal of merit to me, Mr. Wrigley; any views, Mr. Chivers?'

The mine manager hesitated. He wanted to say that every bastard around the table was going over the top – and for what? There was probably some vendetta going off behind the scenes and the murder was fuck-all to do with the pit. The whole enquiry would take days. There would be a mountain of production lost and he would get it in the neck again from the mine owners. If the pit lost money and closed, everybody and his dog would lose their jobs. The police ought to have better things to do. There were real criminals in Derby and Nottingham – running prostitution, gambling dens and getting involved in bank robberies. This was all small fry – who the fuck was Joey Murphy anyway? 'It all seems like a good idea to me Inspector,' he said, lying through his teeth.

'How long will it take to get your inspectors across, Mr. Wrigley?'

'Maybe two hours, Inspector.'

'Good, Sergeant Pollard will get some police support here by then and I'm sure you can provide staff to help us see this through, Mr. Chivers?'

'I'm sure I can,' said Chivers, trying to hide a sinking heart.

'Good, then,' responded Maddox, 'let's try to get all our staff to meet here in about two hours and we'll give them their orders and get things moving.'

CHAPTER TEN

The clock on the small living room mantelpiece ticked with monotonous energy. The first fire of the day, made at daybreak, had burnt back to a warm black and grey mass in the fire-grate with fringes of red and orange occasionally flaking to ash as they burnt. The room was warm and cosy. Lily Daykin was dosing on the small, neat, brown settee under the window when there was a knock on the front door; it was Mrs. Lacey.

'Come in, Mrs. Lacey. Sorry, I was dozing I'm afraid.'

'Thank you my dear, are you feeling any better? I know it's always a shock when you hear of a death, particularly when it involves somebody being killed at the pit. We've all got relations working down that mine and it's just a nightmare when something like this happens. I don't know what his poor wife must be going through, and as for his boys, well they're going to carry that loss for the rest of their lives.'

Lily Daykin did her best to show some detached concern but it was hard. She spoke distantly and quietly.

'I know.' She needed to maintain some continuity of dialogue or she would break down. 'Richard works at the pit as you know Mrs. Lacey, and even though we're divorced, I still shudder when I hear of a fatal accident there. Seems like there is one every year. I remember when we were still married and he'd be late from work. He always worked early afternoons you know and if he wasn't back for ten o' clock at night, I'd start panicking – by half past ten, I'd be frantic. Occasionally, the swine would go straight to the Black Swan and not let me know. He'd roll in about half past eleven just when I was about to go down to the telephone box in the black of night to ring the pit. He could be very selfish and uncaring.'

Then out of the blue with a slightly searching tone:

'Did you know this Joey Murphy, Lily?' The question came as a bombshell. There was an acute need to maintain inner control.

Lily Daykin looked at Mrs. Lacey and tried to gauge whether she was asking a question she already knew the answer to or was making an innocent enquiry. It was difficult to judge. Some elderly people in their acquired wisdom manage to ask or comment in such a manner that they are able to disguise their underlying knowledge, feelings or intentions. She looked directly into Mrs. Lacey's face. 'No, I don't think so. As you know, I sometimes give some of the men that come out of the drift a cup of tea when it's cold, or a cold drink in summer – but I don't think I know this Joey by name, not like I know some of them.' The lie was difficult to conceal but it was the best she could do.

Mrs. Lacey never blinked an eye – wisdom fully engaged.

'No, I don't think I know him either,' she responded, 'and I didn't think I knew his wife either but Maggie next door described her to me. If it is who I think it is, I might have seen her at Ilkeston Market on occasions with her two boys.

Beautiful creatures they are and she's stunning. They say the funeral's next Wednesday, will you be going? Most of the village will be there.'

Lily detected an added element of enquiry in Mrs. Lacey's voice; she was searching for a reaction. 'No, I can't make it, my dad's got a hospital appointment in Nottingham next Wednesday and I need to be with him, you know how poorly he is.'

The old lady hesitated to see whether the younger woman would continue with her dialogue. She didn't.

'OK my love, I'm not going to stop, just wanted to make sure you were feeling better, lots of ironing to do.'

Mrs. Lacey took her leave by the front door. As Lily closed the door behind her, her heart was pounding quietly and her mind was racing and confused. What did the old lady know? What had she seen? What had she heard through the thin walls? She slumped back onto the settee in deep despair, brought both hands to her face and sobbed quietly behind them. This was one of the worst days of her life.

In her grief, Lily fell into a shallow sleep. About half an hour later she was startled back to consciousness by a violent knock at the front door. She opened the door to see her former husband Richard Daykin standing there in a sickening rage, his eyes grimaced half closed and his lips wet with saliva and hatred. 'Heard the news, bitch? Your lover boy's been killed at the pit, ton of rock crushed the bastard, got everything he deserved. Serves you right for divorcing me, God always gets his own back, you filthy whore.' Lily slammed the door closed and bolted the lock. Her heart was beating out of her chest and for the second time in two days she fainted like a sack of coal.

CHAPTER ELEVEN

The small conference room was functional with a grey laminated table and six steel-framed chairs. Three detectives sat to one side of the table headed by Inspector Maddox and two policemen opposite, Sergeant Pollard and Constable John Stevenson. The sixth chair was at the head of the table near to the entrance door. All the officers rose to their feet when Chief Inspector Mike Collins walked in.

'Good morning gentlemen.' Collins sat down and the rest followed. 'So, Joey Murphy, where are we Brian?'

Detective Brian Maddox had prepared his feedback. 'Chief, what seemed in the scheme of things to be fairly simple has now left us grappling a little bit. We know that Joey Murphy was the last to walk down the return gate from the coal face. Apparently, when all the men were about 100 yards from the coal face, Joe remembered he had left his water bottle. He turned round and went back for it. This left the rest of the men about 150 to 200 yards in front of him and still walking out of the mine. Within about two minutes, they had joined the men from the intake roadway at a junction and other men joined and intermingled from a development part of the mine. They all ambled to the shaft bottom and none of them recall seeing Joey again.'

'Does this mean that there was nobody else on Piper 10's district?' asked Collins.

'No,' said Maddox. 'We know that Richard Daykin had gone onto the district via the return roadway at about 1.30pm, he works a sort of early afternoon shift. His job is to drill the coal face in readiness for the next day. The reason he goes on early is that he can work on the face before the coal undercutting men get there on the normal afternoon shift. Once the newly exposed coal face is undercut, all the coal cutting fines build up and that would prevent the driller getting easy access to do his work. The coal cutting men, and there are two of them, entered the face about one hour after Daykin had arrived.'

'So was it only Richard Daykin on the district from about 1.30pm onwards, until the cutter men got there?' asked the chief inspector.

'No, Deputy John Hulme was also on Piper 10's face by about 2.00pm. He's the afternoon shift deputy. He'd gone onto the district via the main intake roadway and crawled along the face, making an inspection. He came across Daykin at the return end of the coal face at about 2.30pm, Daykin had drilled about six holes by that time.'

The chief inspector needed more clarity. 'So all the dayshift men at the return end of the face left via the Piper 10's return roadway at about 1.00pm. Joey Murphy was about 200 yards, two or three minutes behind them we think, having gone back for his water bottle. The men from the return roadway joined with the men from the intake roadway at the outer junction at about 1.15pm and other men joined them from other districts for their walk out of the mine to the shaft bottom. None of them saw Joey Murphy again. Richard Daykin has told you that he entered the return roadway going towards the face at about 1.30pm, he said he did not see Joey Murphy. Are you sure that Daykin would not have come across Murphy?'

'We can't be absolutely sure, Chief,' said Detective Maddox, 'but that's the story we're getting and we haven't got any other evidence at this stage to prove anybody a liar.'

'Well, it seems to me that there can only be a limited number of suspects, the mine is too well controlled for everybody and his dog to be walking about willy-nilly. Daykin seems to have had the best opportunity to have come across Murphy but Deputy Hulme was there or thereabouts and the two cutter men might have seen him, have we got statements from all of them?'

'We have Chief,' responded Maddox, 'but as yet we can't determine who, if any of them, is lying.'

'Well, one or more of them must be. Keep probing gentlemen, make them sweat, one of them must give something away at some time or other, we ought to be getting this case wrapped up in no time, the pressure's on.' The chief inspector continued, 'What do forensics have to say?'

'They have little or nothing to go on, boss,' said Maddox. 'Joey's body was thick black with sweat and coal dust and there are no discernible fingerprints. After he had been wiped down, there was some bruising to the back of the neck but the most obvious injuries are the two deep and bloodied imprints to the front of the neck. The poor bugger was strangled but whoever did it must have been using gloves. There are no fingerprints and the indentations are broader than the normal thumb width. The murderer must have been wearing the thick leather gloves, the sort that are used by all the colliers.'

'Where do they keep their gloves?' asked the Chief.

'Well, as far as I can see,' said Sergeant Pollard, 'they either wear them, or tuck them into their belts or down their shirts when they are working or moving about underground. When they come out of the mine, I imagine they'll be thrown into their lockers with all their other pit clothes ready for the next shift.'

'Have we searched any of the lockers as yet?'

'No.'

'Well,' said the Chief Inspector, 'you'd better get to it. Start with Daykin's, Hulme's and the two cutter men's, it's a long shot but you never know.'

Chapter Twelve

The No.1 Derby Crown Court room was crowded. The case of Rex v Daykin was in its fifth and final day.

Judge Abraham Close looked across at the jury. 'Members of the jury, have you reached a verdict?'

A small man on the left of the jury panel rose to his feet. 'We have, your honour.'

'And what is it, guilty or not guilty?'

'We find the defendant guilty, your honour.'

'Thank you, members of the jury,' responded the judge, 'you may sit down Mr. Foreman.'

The judge turned to Richard Daykin who was standing forlornly in the dock.

'Richard Michael Daykin, you have been found guilty of the murder of Joseph Peter Murphy, collier of this county. The evidence that has been presented to this court is irrefutable. A number of witnesses have testified that, notwithstanding you are a divorcee, you remain extremely jealous of your former wife and of any associations that she has had with the opposite sex since your divorce. Two persons have testified that they have seen Joey Murphy visit the home of your former wife, Mrs. Lily Daykin, on more than one occasion, and during each visit, the bedroom curtains were closed while he was there, albeit for only very short periods of time. One person has testified that he was aware of what was going on and he had informed you, although mockingly, weeks before the murder took place. You had bided your time. Every working day, you would have passed Joseph Murphy as he came out of the mine and you travelled in. He would not have realised that you were looking out for him.

'On the fateful day in question, Joey Murphy was delayed from the normal group of his working colleagues, having returned to the coal face to collect his water bottle. When you entered the return roadway, Joey Murphy was walking towards you all by himself. You attacked him in a jealous rage and strangled him to death. You dragged his body the twenty yards or so into Henshaw's Drift and then you attempted to conceal his body by pulling down some of the fragile roof with a pick or some other tool. You then cold-bloodedly continued your journey into the mine and commenced your normal work of drilling the coal face where you were next seen by Deputy Hulme. But you made one big mistake. You retained the leather work gloves that you had on your person, on your hands, when you strangled Joseph Murphy to death. It was only when you got out of the mine into the brightly lit baths that you realised there were blood stains on the tips of the thumbs of the gloves. You threw them into the bottom of your dirty locker and hoped to dispose of them secretly when you were able.'

'But you were foiled by the good work of the police. They had decided to search several lockers of the leading suspects and they found your work gloves before you had time to dispose of them. The blood on those gloves was analysed forensically and was found to be that of Joseph Murphy's blood type. You murdered him in an opportunistic and vicious jealous rage. You cared not for him or his wife or his children but for your own jealous and gratuitous revenge. For this heinous crime, I sentence you to capital punishment. You will be taken from this court to Nottingham Prison and, on a date to be set, you will be hanged by the neck until you are dead. Take him down.'

Before the court constables had time to move in, Richard Daykin screamed out. 'I didn't do it. Please listen to me, I didn't do it.' The constables moved in with additional force and grabbed Daykin. 'I tell you, your honour, I didn't do it.' He was now fighting off the court constables. 'Yes I was jealous but that whore was seeing anybody and everybody. She was no longer my wife but she still knew I loved her with a passion. Why did she do this to me? Why didn't she have me back? She's caused all this but I swear to God, I didn't kill Joey Murphy.'

'Take him down,' said the judge forcibly. Daykin was dragged, kicking and screaming like an animal, to the cells below.

Chapter Thirteen

It was 10.15pm and Mary Murphy was alone in her small living room, sitting on a simple settee and gazing into the dying embers of a coal fire. Her two boys were asleep upstairs. It had been ten weeks since she had received the fateful news of the death of her husband in such horrible circumstances. The arrest of the murderer and his trial had all happened so quickly. In one week's time, he would receive the punishment he deserved.

In the interim there had been unbelievable comfort and succour from her immediate family and friends. She and the boys had been carried through the ordeal of the funeral. Her mother and father had done all that they could – being there, visiting almost every day, having the boys, making meals – all the things that keep a person going when near insanity is making its call and wanting to wreak havoc. Her brother Brian had made all the funeral arrangements, dealt with minor financial matters, applied for state help and sorted out the small entitlements she was due from the pit owners. Soon there would be little or no money to carry them through – but she would make it with the help of her near and extended family and all the caring neighbours around her. There was no telling yet what the shock would do to the boys, but one thing was certain; she in turn would always be there for them. It was going to be a hard life from now on in.

Her feelings of despair were tainted with anger. She had never realised that her husband could have been so deceitful, so unfaithful. For years her marriage had been absolute bliss and the gift of two beautiful boys had been the icing on the cake. God's gift, two boys in their own image, healthy, strong, exciting – and all that made life worth living for. And now her husband – an adulterer.

There was a gentle knock at the kitchen door. Mary was a little startled; it was just turning dark, a filthy night with heavy rain.

'Who is it?'

There was a quiet voice of a woman – 'It's me Mrs. Murphy, Lily Daykin.'

'Daykin?' Mary's heart immediately began to pound with uncontrollable shock. She regained some control.

'Daykin – the whore? What a cheek you have, coming anywhere near my house. Please go away immediately, you common filthy bitch.' Mary shocked herself by the manner and tone she had instinctively adopted – it was alien to her nature and upbringing, but the circumstances had overridden her natural courtesy and dignity. She was completely out of character, driven by overriding grief and unbelievable inner psychological pain.

'I need to speak to you Mrs. Murphy, it's important.'

'How dare you speak of importance to me you common harlot. What was important to me is now dead.'

'It's that that I want to speak to you about Mrs. Murphy – I know this can't be easy for you – but two rights don't make a wrong – there is something not real about all that has happened – we need to speak – please – please let me in.'

'No way.'

'Mrs. Murphy – I know what I did was wrong – I wish it had never happened. More than ever now, I wish it had never happened – I wouldn't have wished this on my own worst enemy.' A pause. 'But these things do happen Mrs. Murphy – it wasn't planned – it came out of the blue for me too. You must understand, I didn't go looking for your husband, we met by chance – all this is agony for me too.'

'You haven't a clue what agony is. Being without a husband is agony, being without a father is agony, losing a son before his time is agony – that's agony Daykin – that's agony.'

'Mrs Murphy – please let me in.'

Mary drooped her back to the door. What was now happening couldn't be real either. Her husband had been murdered. His adultery had come out in court. The woman he had bedded was now outside her house – at gone ten o'clock at night – pleading to come into her house – her home – to talk to her, to look into her face, to see her eyes, to see the eyes of the wife whose husband she had bedded. What a bastard. What a cheating, lying, bare-faced bastard – how could any woman have such audacity to present herself in such a manner and in such circumstances?

But Mary's mind drifted on – her thoughts now mangled and complex. *Who is this woman? What is she like, what does she look like; is she beautiful, had she performed in bed with my husband better than I could? What did they speak of before and after sex – did it take long – how often did it happen – was it leading anywhere, did he love her more than he loved me?* Mary closed her eyes, continued to lean backwards on the front door, wished for a second that she was dead, her feelings now in such a pit of despair and hatred.

'Mrs. Murphy – please let me in.'

'No.'

'Mrs. Murphy – please let me in.'

'Please go, you cannot imagine what hurt you are causing me. For God's sake go.'

'Mrs. Murphy, there has been a miscarriage of justice. An innocent man is going to be hung. This cannot be right. Please Mrs. Murphy, please let me in.'

Mary closed her eyes and wished that the world would swallow her up. If it wasn't for the children, she thought, she would like to go from this earth – disappear – leave everything behind without mark or trace – go for good – go forever.

But her conscience now felt a twinge. What on earth could this woman mean? Surely she didn't think her ex-husband was innocent – and why should she? The bastard had been unfaithful to her apparently – surely she couldn't forgive him – or forgive the murder he had committed.

'Mrs. Murphy – we need to speak – we must speak – you would not want to be party to an injustice – you cannot let an innocent man die.'

'He's guilty, beyond all reasonable doubt, that's what the jury concluded. You're just guilty that you helped cause all this, it's your guilty mind that's brought you here.'

'Mrs. Murphy, please, please let me in.'

There was silence – a long silence. Pleas and exchanges had come to an end. Another pause, another silence. The door clicked open quietly, the two women looked at each other –

both beautiful, both distressed – one extremely angry, the other exuding remorsefulness.

'Come in if you must,' said Mary coldly.

The two women stood in the kitchen looking at each other, each trying to make sense of what was happening, trying to make a first judgement of whom they were looking at, trying to make normal what was completely abnormal.

'You had better come through to the front room,' said Mary, hardly believing what she was doing. 'Sit down,' she said coldly. Mary glanced her hand towards the armchair. Lily Daykin sat down – elegantly, quietly, embarassingly.

The two women made slow but determined eye contact. Mary was determined to outstare her assailant if it were at all possible. She had nothing to hide, nothing to feel guilty about, nothing to be ashamed of. Lily Daykin looked at Mary with equal determination but with a sorrowful gaze. There was another lull while each woman endeavoured to determine what on earth could be said next. The silence continued, almost excruciatingly.

'So,' said Mary, 'what is it that has given you the cheek to come here of all places? Here, where your lover boy lived – with me – with his sons – here – in this home – where we made our lives together – where we had dreams together – where we, or rather I – now – then – where we thought we would grow old together. Have you come to gloat? Do you have some perverted desire to see me – here – here in my loneliness – here in my despair – destroyed – betrayed – living each pain of every day? Thinking of what might have been – what should have been – is this what you came to see?'

'No, Mrs. Murphy.'

'Then, what is it then? What is it that you want? What on earth is it that I could say or do to even begin to help anyone about anything? And why should I? I'm the injured party, me, me and my boys – they will have their lives changed forever. And why? Because of their father, their father, and his rotten infidelity – with you – you who have ruined everything – you – you – sitting here – here in my living room – my living room – mine – here. This is all because of you.'

'I really am truly sorry Mrs. Murphy – truly sorry.'

'Truly sorry? Truly. Sorry. Really sorry. Really truly sorry. Wishing I could turn the clock back sorry. Wish this had never happened sorry. Sorry from the bottom of my heart sorry. Truly sorry. Truly. Sorry – sorry – but who are you sorry for Mrs. Daykin? No, don't tell me. I know who you are sorry for – you're sorry for yourself – you – yourself – truly sorry. Truly. Sorry. For yourself.' Mary was near to tears.

'I am truly sorry for you, Mrs. Murphy.'

'So there we are then. You're truly sorry for me. For me. Not for you, for me. Well fancy that. You're truly sorry for me. For me. For me, who's lost her husband, her life, her happiness, her dignity, her soul, her will to live. You know what, that's very kind of you Mrs. Daykin, that's really kind of you. And to think, if you hadn't flirted with my husband, you know, flirted – you know – bedded – if you hadn't bedded my husband you wouldn't have needed to feel sorry. And just think, if he hadn't been murdered – why – you could have gone on bedding him – you know – fucking him – you know – you could have gone on forever – fucking him – fucking him while I was here – here in this home – waiting with the boys – waiting for him to come home – you know – after he'd fucked you.'

There was a long pause. Lily Daykin could see that she had destroyed a life – lives. She wasn't proud of herself; she had not meant this to happen. She had been party to a catastrophe – a human catastrophe – a nightmare – she had caused it – this was all her fault. The woman in front of her – sitting on her own settee – in her own living room – in her own home – with her own children upstairs – in their own bedroom – sleeping – this woman in front of her was utterly distraught – and she had caused it. If it were ever possible in this world to undo the things that one has done wrong, this would be the time. The time to have gone back, closed the door, said "no", to have turned away, to have not taken the deviation that led to this scenario – if it were only possible to undo things – if it were only possible. But now it was too late; the dye had been cast. She had succumbed to temptation, to flattery, to another man's desires – to her desires – to her loneliness – and it was too late to turn back. Lily Daykin took a deep breath.

'Mrs. Murphy, what I did was wrong, I know that. I shouldn't have done it. It was wrong – and yet – and yet – it happened and I couldn't help it.' Lily Daykin was trying not to make excuses. 'It sometimes happens. One minute you're going about your daily life, sometimes you're daily boring life and then "bang" – it happens – something happens in your life and the world turns upside down. You don't plan it, you don't think about it, you consider something like that could never happen and then, there you are – washing the pots or scrubbing the floor or making the bed or, or – and then – bang.'

'Oh! So it's as simple as that is it? I didn't realise, I thought other men belonged to other women – you know – men, women, husbands, wives – you know – this is my   wife –

you know – my wife – I married her you know – she's mine. And this is my husband – you know – the man I married – said some vows – you know – he said something about "forsaking all others" and – let me see – you would have said the same thing – wouldn't you – you know – about your own husband – once – didn't you? Well, didn't you?'

Lily Daykin stared forward in deep contemplation. Everything that Mary Murphy was saying was right. Her marriage, her vows, the plans they had had, her and her husband – and children – no – there were no children – thank God there were no children. They had wanted children – perhaps a boy and a girl – definitely more than one – more than one child – yes, a boy and a girl would have been just right. But they couldn't have children, there was a problem, children never turned up, she didn't get pregnant – her fault apparently – the doctor said it was her fault – apparently – couldn't happen – wouldn't happen. Not sure that fault was the right word – why should it be someone's fault – does someone have to take the blame – is it a fault – was it her fault? It probably was – yes it was, she remembers now – the sperm was rich enough – but where was the egg? That was the question – the egg – there was no egg – or if there was the bastard wouldn't reveal itself – to the sperm that is – reveal itself to the sperm. And there was plenty of sperm. Every night there was plenty of sperm – released in passion, in desire – making demented young love – every night – and still no baby. And years past and still sperm, less sperm now – but enough – enough sperm – enough to make a thousand babies – but something's not working – not clicking – enough sperm for a thousand babies and still no babies – no babies.

'Well – didn't you?' said Mary Murphy.

'Sorry, didn't I what?'

'Make vows forsaking all others – both of you – you and your husband – make vows – forsaking all others.'

Lily Daykin's eyes glazed over – 'We did. We did. Forsaking all others – 'til death do us part. We did.'

Another silence. Mary Murphy was turning the screw, inflicting pain on her unwelcome visitor – sweet revenge – as long as it would last. 'So you couldn't have children?'

'No.'

'Good. Bastards like you don't deserve children – lying, selfish, immoral bastards like you – don't deserve children – too fucking selfish to deserve children. Why should people like you have children – you probably wouldn't know who the father was anyway – if you had had children – anybody's children – how would you know who the father is – was – how would you know?'

Silence.

'How long had it been going on for?' Mary's blunt question shocked Lily Daykin. A knife in the shoulder blades could not have been more penetrating.

'Sorry?' She responded with a hesitation that some more pain would now be out.

Mary stared at the other woman with courageous defiance. 'So how long had this affair been going on for? You know, how long had you been seeing my husband – you know – fucking him. How long had you been fucking him Mrs. Daykin?' Lily Daykin's blood began to drain; whatever she said would be an admission of sinful guilt, actions that she had taken that had ruined the life of the woman in front of her.

More silence.

'I only knew him for three months before he was killed. He'd been one of the men who had come out of Henshaw's Drift from time to time. There was always one deputy and one workman; apparently the drift had to be inspected every thirty days or something. He was always with a deputy. Occasionally I would see them and offer a drink – to any of the men – I was just being friendly. They always seemed tired and bedraggled; I was just being friendly.'

'I still don't understand how you finished up in bed with my husband.' Mary was almost intrigued.

'Neither do I, not really.' Another long pause. 'It was one Saturday afternoon, about three o'clock. There was a knock at my back door. I opened it and their stood your Joseph. I was startled to see him. I could hardly recognise him in his clean day clothes, I had only previously seen him in his pit clothes – black and dusty. He looked different. I asked him what he wanted. "Is the kettle on?" he said. I didn't know how to respond. What on earth does a woman do when a relative stranger, albeit someone you had spoken to before, but only in passing, stands at your door and asks if the kettle is on?'

'So what did you do?' Mary needed to know. Painful as any anticipated response might be, Mary needed to know.

'I told him to come in. I knew in an instant that what I had said was innately wrong. A woman does not invite a relative stranger into her home. I had initiated one of the worst mistakes of my life – just like that – just by saying "come in". Two little words – two little words that were to destroy so many people's lives. Mrs. Murphy,' (hesitatingly) 'Mary, I didn't know it would all lead to this – it was not of

79

my original making – I had planned nothing – if I had not seen Joseph ever again, it would have meant nothing to me – I didn't know the man at all really.'

'But you obviously got to know him.'

'Yes, I got to know him – I'm sorry.'

'Well, go on then. Tell me how you got to know him – tell me how it got from a cup of tea to the bedroom. Christ it's a long way from a cup of tea to the bedroom. Tell me, tell me for God's sake.'

Lily Daykin stared at the poor demented soul before her, her stare drifting deeper and deeper, her eyes fixated and glazed, focussed and unfocussed, seeing and not seeing. 'I made a cup of tea for us both,' she said. 'We – that is – I, was uneasy, about everything – and he was obviously unnerved and yet determined. We drank our tea, the tea was irrelevant – we drank our tea and both of us knew that we were doing something wrong. We drank our tea and then I could feel his longing gaze, a gaze that would not avert itself. I asked him, "Why have you come here?" He answered – "Don't you think that's obvious – to see you?" I asked him – "Why to see me – you don't know me?" He said that he couldn't put me out of his mind – I'd given him and others a drink when they had come out of the mine but that had set a rabbit running for him. He said he had to see me, he said he knew he was doing wrong but he couldn't, wouldn't be diverted.'

'So that's what he said, did he?' Mary was aching inside. 'Well that's a pretty ordinary line to take isn't it – couldn't get you out of his mind eh? I wonder where me and his two sons were at this point in time – you know – in his mind – in his mind that he couldn't get *you* out of – would there be any room for me and the kids in his mind at that time, or did you – you – did you fully occupy his mind? You know fully. When he was here, here with us, would it have been the case that he wasn't actually here – here with us because you – you – you were filling his mind. He would be talking to us and thinking only of you. His boys would be asking a question and he'd answer but the answer was false, shallow – because his thoughts were not on the question but only on you – you who apparently was filling his mind.'

'Mary?' Lily Daykin uttered her response pitifully, forlornly, almost begging some inverted sympathy because of the dilemma she was confronting.

'Don't you dare call me Mary – how dare you call me Mary – am I supposed to be your sister or something? Have you now been with me long enough to cause you to exercise familiarity – with me – the woman whose husband you have bedded? The woman with whose husband you committed a sinful act that has not only resulted in his death but has also destroyed me and has caused your ex-husband to commit murder out of jealousy and who will now hang for it – three lives ruined, just at the drop of a hat – or should I say at the drop of your knickers – you filthy bitch.'

Lily Daykin looked pitifully at the woman in front of her. She could see Mary's pain in every sinew of her face and body, in every look and every movement. Contorted pain, psychological pain, unbelievable pain, pain that is hard for anyone to imagine. This was real pain, the pain of a woman destroyed – destroyed by events – events for which she had been the uncaring, selfish catalyst.

'Everything that you say is understandable but you don't really mean what you are saying, do you Mrs. Murphy? It's not you to be vindictive is it? I know what you are saying is said out of pain, I understand your despair.'

'You understand nothing you filthy bitch, nothing.' A long pause – Mary Murphy was not used to using harsh or foul language under normal circumstances – the despair and betrayal had caused her to step out of character. Such was her mountain of bitterness that she was no longer the epitome of politeness and decency that had, until now, been an innate part of her make-up. 'Please get out of my house.'

Lily Daykin needed to continue; there was a purpose in her mission and it wasn't for personal gain. 'Mrs. Murphy, Richard Daykin did not kill your husband. I know him better than anybody. Yes, he was an adulterer, a bastard to me at times with his irritation in not having children, but he also had a gentle side; he never used violence against anyone, not me, not anyone. He couldn't cold-bloodedly kill anything let alone another human being.'

'And do you think that provides him with a defence?' asked Mary coldly. 'Because you think he is a gentle person, is that defence enough? They proved what he did in court. He was the only one to have seen my husband after he got delayed that day, you know yourself he remained jealous of your associations – even though you were divorced. But more than that, his gloves had my husband's blood on them, he'd hidden them like a common murderer to avoid being caught. He killed my husband out of jealousy and the root cause of that jealousy was you, Daykin, you and your loose morals and infidelities. Please get out of my house.'

'Mrs. Murphy, Richard said he had lost his gloves about three days before Joey's murder. He says he was set up somehow, he doesn't know how – but I believe him. Much as I hate him for what he did to me, I cannot see an innocent man hung for a crime he didn't commit. Is there anything you can think of Mrs. Murphy, anything that Joey might have said before his death that might shine some light on who his true killer might be?'

'You seem to have extremely shallow reasons for thinking that your former husband is innocent,' responded Mary. 'As far as I am concerned, the evidence was incontrovertible, and there was nothing, nothing at all that Joey said or did that indicated he knew what was coming to him, nothing.'

'Are you sure?' pleaded Lily Daykin.

'I'm more than sure – I'm positive – now please get out of my house.'

Lily Daykin raised herself to her feet in defeat. She looked at Mary and then lowered her head disdainfully. She walked slowly to the front door and opened it herself. It was still teeming with rain outside. She pulled her shawl half over her head and turned to Mary Murphy, who had followed almost directly behind in a manner that wanted to ease her unwelcome visitor out of her house as quickly as possible. As Lily Daykin passed over the threshold, she turned to Mary and looked directly into her troubled face. 'There's one more thing you should know, Mrs. Murphy, before I leave you.'

Mary responded scornfully, 'Oh really – and what's that?'

'I know it doesn't show much, you haven't noticed have you?'

There was an induced pause.

'I'm actually six months pregnant.'

Then another deathly silent pause.

'Good night, Mrs. Murphy.'

Chapter Fourteen

The early morning sun came streaming through the window and fell upon Mary Murphy's face as she sat dozing on the settee. It was 6.45am. She hadn't made it to her bed. The events of the previous evening with Lily Daykin had upset her beyond belief and she had cried herself to sleep. Mary started to stir and her thoughts immediately began to drift to the nightmare circumstances that had prevailed only a few hours before. The boys were still fast asleep upstairs.

Mary's thoughts were running away with her. How on earth could a woman who had committed adultery with her husband turn up at her front door? A woman whose actions had led to a train of events that resulted in Lily Daykin's ex-husband killing Joey in a jealous rage. How could Lily Daykin have possibly brought herself to come to the house, knowing that she was the cause of all the pain that had now afflicted so many peoples' lives? It all seemed like a bad dream – a dream that she would have given every penny not to be true. And Lily Daykin was so unbelievably sure that her ex-husband was not guilty of the murder, despite the overwhelming evidence in court and her own flimsy reasons for believing in his innocence. She still believed him to be innocent despite his own adultery and his jealous rages.

Mary eased herself up from the settee and made her way to the kitchen. She lit the small gas ring, half-filled the kettle and placed it slowly onto the blue flame. Her mind was confused but her thoughts were still racing and the thought that was so predominant in her mind – how could her husband have been so deceitful? How was it that he had apparently been committing adultery for two to three months and she had not known a single thing about what was going on? She tried to think back. Did his behaviour ever once suggest that he was seeing another woman? The answer was "no"; there had not been a single thing out of the ordinary either with his demeanour, his habits or his timetable. In point of fact, he had been even more attentive than usual on some days – had all this been a smokescreen?

The kettle boiled and Mary made tea. Life was very lonely now, very different. Previously she would have felt Joey wrench himself from their bed each work morning, dress in almost darkness, ease himself out of the bedroom and downstairs and off to the pit. She would stay in their warm bed for another hour, half asleep, half awake. Then she would rise herself and prepare for the hectic wakening of the boys, ensuring they came downstairs in good time, helping them dress, feeding them and sending them off to school with all the neighbourhood kids. Now it was her that reacted to the alarm clock and forced herself out of bed and forced herself to wake the boys and forced herself to dress them and a forced a smile as they left for school. Everything was forced, forced – not because she loved or cared for the boys any less – but forced because there was no one to share them with, no one to walk out with, go to church with, laugh with – as adults laugh. Her boys were the world to her but that world had encompassed a loving husband – the old world was made up of four people and now there were only three – one corner of the loving stability block was missing.

Mary said her goodbyes as the boys left for school. She closed the door behind them with a lump in her throat and a heart wanting to ache out of her chest. This was the worst moment of each day – she was alone with the realisation that Joey was no longer working at the coal face on their behalf, stripped to the waist with a beautiful, black sweat-glistening torso hurling coal onto a conveyor with all his might – for their sakes, for their livelihood. The boys would be coming home from school but Joey would not be trundling in before them or after them. They would not be having a normal family meal ever again – the four of them – satisfying their appetite, laughing, rib-taking, planning what to do next – how to have fun – that had all now gone. She couldn't take the boys fishing, or play proper football with them or make bows and arrows or bowl a googly – that had all gone. Everything had gone from the father-son relationship because the father had gone – murdered in cold blood by a jealous maniac.

Mary busied herself as best she could. Beds to make, some washing to catch up on, vegetables to prepare, sink and toilet to scrub. The work took twice as long and appeared to be twice as difficult as it used to be, when Joey was alive and when he would be coming home to see the fruits of her endeavours. She was thinking to herself: *when the purpose of one's life – or much of it – has left your life, everything seems an uphill struggle, never to be properly fulfilled again. How much do we take for granted in our lives – how stupid can one be not to grasp every benefit,*

86

every blessing that we have, every day, all the time – a husband, sons, an extended family, friends – all taken for granted? Why is it that we moan so quickly when life does not take exactly the course we want it to? Why do our responses exude superficiality at the drop of hat, just because some minor deflection does not fit into our plans? All these scenarios and arguments cycled through Mary's mind as she forced herself to do her daily chores – her daily, boring, repetitive chores.

Fortunately, today, her boredom would be eased, her mind occupied, thanks to a routine visit by her mother. Margaret Smith was one of those women whose family was the be-all and end-all of her life; she had innate loyalty to each and every one of them and now that she had a daughter in trouble, it was her duty to help cushion the pain and stabilise the circumstances. She was also punctual and knocked and entered her daughter's house at exactly twelve noon. They kissed and embraced – how thankful Mary Murphy was that she had the best mother and father in the world – and how many times had she taken them both for granted?

'How are you dear, have the boys gone off to school?'

'They have Mum, and I'm fine – well – as well as can be expected.' Mary tried to put on a brave face but her mother was not persuaded.

'It still hurts doesn't it sweetheart, it will hurt for a long time yet, but the hurt will recede – one day. I know it doesn't seem like that yet but it will – one day, not yet – not soon – but one day.'

'So you keep saying, Mum, and I hope you're right. But even if life does get better, it won't answer the question as to why he felt the need to go off with another woman. What is it that I have done wrong, how have I let him down, why wasn't I good enough for him, what was my inadequacy?' Mary paused. 'And you know how I felt about him Mum, I loved him more than life itself, I lived for him, gave him two sons and loved them all beyond measure. What is it that a woman has to do to hold on to her husband, to prove to him that he and his boys are all I lived for?'

'Life can be strange and unbelievably cruel,' responded the saddened mother. 'I really don't know what goes through some men's minds; they seem to have everything but they seem to be dictated to by what's in their trousers. It seems that nature programmes half of them to look for satisfaction elsewhere, not for love but for satisfaction – not even satisfaction – self-gratification – that's what they're looking for – self-gratification; it's pitiful, more than that, hurtful – downright hurtful. They want their cake and they want to eat it; by some strange force of nature they are prepared to risk everything for their male entrenched self-gratification.'

'I never thought Joey was like that Mum, I never realised, I still can't believe it.'

'No, neither can I Mary, I thought he was the most wonderful son-in-law in the world. This has come as a total surprise to me – and to your father.'

'How is Dad, Mum?'

'He's completely bewildered and completely destroyed at this present moment in time. I have never seen him so tearful. He thought the world of Joey as you know, he was like a second son to him – he can't believe what has happened – what with how he has treated you and what it's all led to.'

'And what about you, Mum?'

'Me – well I need to be strong – for you, for your father, for my grandsons; no point in me giving up the ghost – that wouldn't do at all. And then there's poor Brian – he looked on Joey as though they were brothers – he's not the same; he broods, he's listless, it'll take some time for him to get over everything as well.'

There was a pause.

'Mum, have you ever lost anyone very close to you?'

Margaret Smith gazed into the distance. There was a long, vacant, painful pause. 'Yes,' she said quietly.

'Grandma and Grandad?'

'Well them obviously, but you do get over your parents' death, especially if they have lived a long and fulfilling life – as your grandparents did. Your Grandma was eighty-three when she died and Grandad was seventy-seven – that's not a bad life as things go – better than average.'

'You said obviously, was there someone else?' Mary enquired.

Another distant gaze formed on Margaret Smith's face and a semblance of a tear started to glisten from the corner of one eye. There was a reluctance in her mannerisms, as though she did not want to divulge anything – and yet she had been asked a straightforward question from a loved one that, maybe, deserved a candid answer. She responded quietly and with some deliberation but mixed with hesitation. 'Before I married your father, there was another man – a boyfriend really.'

Mary was startled. 'Another man – I didn't know.'

'No, you wouldn't know. I've never told you, you didn't need to know. It was before I met your father. We were madly in love but something awful happened.'

'Awful, what do you mean awful?' Mary was intrigued but almost frightened at the same time.

'Well we were both very young, I was eighteen and he was nineteen. He appeared to be a very gentle person, I never saw him lose his temper, not once. He came from a farming background. One day, completely out of the blue, he went berserk at another man he accused of making a pass at me as we were walking along the canal bank. I couldn't believe what I was seeing. He attacked this other poor bloke like a madman and he eventually knocked him flying into the canal. The poor bloke couldn't swim, he screamed out in desperation and lifted his hands towards us to pull him out of the water. My boyfriend simply lashed out at him, kicking his hands and arms away and watching the poor man get even more frantic. All this went on for what seemed like an eternity – only a few minutes I guess, maybe only seconds – and then this poor chap slowly disappeared under the water and I watched him drown before my very eyes – it was the most awful thing I had ever seen.'

'So what did you do?'

'Well there was no one else about. I had seen it all and I was the only witness. He pleaded with me not to say anything, I was in a complete quandary. I kept quiet for nearly a week but my conscience wouldn't let me carry the secret any further and I told the police.'

'And what happened?'

'The police had the canal searched for nearly a week. They couldn't find anything. I was even beginning to question my own sanity. I was asking myself, did I actually see what I'd thought I'd seen or was it all a bad dream? Had the man I'd seen drown before my very eyes not drowned at all? Had he actually survived and we had not known? After all, when he had gone under the water my boyfriend insisted we should scarper – leave the scene as though nothing had happened. We did – it was the most cowardly, distressing thing I had ever done in my life.'

'Mum – you must have been beside yourself. I never knew you had known such agony.'

'There was worse to come. About eight days afterwards, a guy riding along the canal bank on his bicycle smelled a terrible reek. He spotted a body floating in the water and reported it to the police. This corroborated my evidence to them. My then boyfriend was arrested.'

'What happened – was he hung?'

'No, he got off with manslaughter. The police had been advised by their own lawyers, and the defence lawyers also pleaded at the trial that there had been no intention to kill another person, no premeditation, so the prosecution reverted from murder to manslaughter. He was given ten years – after only five months he hung himself in prison. I never saw him after the court case, I had had to be a prosecution witness against someone I had fallen in love with, and even though I had witnessed his terrible assault on a perfectly innocent person, I shed a tear the day I got to know he had killed himself. Life is so tragic sometimes.'

'Why do you think he acted so out of character when he attacked this other bloke?'

'I don't know Mary; his defence argued that he was schizophrenic. They wanted him to be sent to a mental home but the jury wouldn't buy it and he finished up in a normal prison.'

'Good God, Mum – and I never knew – how on earth did you manage to keep all that to yourself – did Dad know?'

'Yes, for lots of reasons your dad knew but we both decided we would never speak about it either to you or your brother or sister. What you didn't know, you didn't know – there was no need for you to know and no need for you to worry about anything. It was all put behind us – like most families, there is at least one skeleton in the cupboard and the fewer that get out the better.'

Mary looked at her mother's doleful demeanour and reminded herself of what a wonderful mother she had. Mary had always recognised her mother's innate strength of character but the revelations she had heard from her today only served to raise her admiration in someone she already adored.

'You never ever complain do you Mum? Whatever life throws at you, you always put others before yourself – you're always there aren't you? What on earth would I do without you?'

'You'd carry on – like we all have to do Mary. Despite the awful thing that has happened to Joey, you've been brought up to know – to recognise – that despite what has happened, life has to carry on for the sake of our children and our grandchildren.'

Mary nodded, she heard what her mother had said but was in no doubt that her own strength of character would never match that of her mother's. It seemed to her that each successive generation had a life that was that bit easier than each previous generation and that her own generation would never have the strength or the dutifulness to match that of her forefathers.

As the two women sat in quiet contemplation, the back door clicked open. There was a voice; it was Mrs. Taylor from next door.

'Hello – it's me.' Mrs. Taylor couldn't wait to get the words out. 'Have you heard the news Mary?'

'What news?' More fears.

'About Lily Daykin – you know – the ex-wife of the swine that killed your Joey – lives in Strelley Grange hamlet – they've found her with her head in the gas oven this morning – dead as a dodo so they say.' There was more. 'And you're not going to believe this, she'd given premature birth during the night, all on her own. By some miracle the baby is still alive, a little boy apparently.'

Chapter Fifteen

The kitchen floor was covered in blood, the baby was struggling for life in an incubator five miles away in Nottingham General Hospital and the police photographers were taking shots, at different angles, of Lily Daykin's pitiful body as it rested with the head thrust into the gas oven. Standing at the front of the house, waiting for the photographers to complete their work, were two ambulance men, a doctor and nurse from the local hospital, the local vicar and neighbour, Mrs. Lacey. At the front garden gate, next to the parked ambulance, were three or four distressed neighbours and a man from the local press.

A car pulled up next to the ambulance; it was Detective Inspector Brian Maddox. He got out of the car slowly, walked to the front door which was partly open, acknowledged the people standing on the front yard with a slight nod of the head and entered the house and then the kitchen with a quiet dignity. He immediately caught sight of Sergeant Pollard.

'How far have we got, Pete?' said the detective inspector.

'Well the first ambulance took the baby away about an hour ago, the photographers have been working for about ten minutes, they should be done shortly. Dr. Evans pronounced death when he arrived about three-quarters of an hour ago, the body hasn't actually been moved.'

'Anything suspicious as yet?' asked Maddox almost apologetically, 'I'm sorry, I normally wouldn't be here but the Chief thought we ought to check all the angles out, taking into account her husband, ex-husband that is, is due for hanging next week.'

'I don't think so, it looks as if the poor girl has given birth on the floor in the living room and then has dragged herself to the kitchen and then to the oven, she must have been in desperate straits – what a tragedy – I've never known anything like this.'

The detective inspector glanced around in the kitchen and sombrely surveyed the scene before him. The photographers were packing their cameras. 'Just hang on a few minutes lads,' said Maddox.

The detective looked around the room. The door between the kitchen and the living room was open and there was a brown-red stain that had been scraped along the kitchen floor tiles emanating from the living room. The trail of blood scraped its way on the tiled floor towards the kitchen cooker. Lily's head was still fully inside the oven between two wire oven shelves, the arms lay limply down by her side and the legs and feet lay angled in unison. Her own knickers were wrapped around her feet and her dress was blood-soaked. Blood was brown and thick on both hands and forearms as though Lily had assisted with the birth in her solitary desperation. There were a number of bloody footprints around the kitchen where the ambulance men, the doctor and nurse and others had all trailed about at the scene.

'Who found the body, Sergeant?'

'I did,' interjected Mrs. Lacey. As the immediate neighbour, the old lady had ventured into the house without hesitation to render whatever assistance she could.

The police sergeant explained. 'Mrs. Lacey is Mrs. Daykin's next-door neighbour, Inspector, they've been neighbours for years.'

'Tell me what happened please, Mrs. Lacey,' said Maddox.

'It was absolutely horrible. I came round this morning about nine o'clock, you know, just to see how she was, I often call in Inspector. I half suspected there might be a bit of a problem.'

'Really, why?'

'Well, she was in very late last night, heard her front door go, must have been nearly twelve o'clock, not like her at all inspector. Anyway, I knocked on her front door this morning and there was no answer. Her bedroom curtains were still open and I hadn't heard her go out or anything. I was just about to turn and go away when I smelt this smell, I knew straight away that it was gas. I went round the back and looked through the kitchen window and I could see Lily on the floor near the gas oven – Inspector, it was absolutely terrifying.'

Seeing that Mrs. Lacey was genuinely upset, the detective held back on his questioning enough for the old lady to regain her composure.

And then, 'Did you send for help?'

'I ran two doors down to Mrs. Brown's and asked her to ring for the police and an ambulance. She's the only one around here that has a telephone,' replied Mrs. Lacey, 'And then, and I know I'm stupid, but as a young woman – believe it or not – I use to be in the WRAC and was trained to deal with all sorts of emergencies, I ran back and opened the kitchen door as far as it would go and let the fresh air get into the place. I probably gave it about sixty seconds, took a deep breath and held it and just went in. As soon as I laid my hands on Lily I knew she had gone – she was cold and lifeless. There was nothing I could do.'

The detective nodded slowly. 'You've been remarkably brave Mrs. Lacey, I'm sure you did everything that was possible. More by the sounds of it.'

A quiet moment. 'And then what happened?' asked Maddox.

'I was next on the scene, Inspector,' interjected Constable Stevenson. 'I went into the house via the back kitchen door; the front was locked. I saw Mrs. Daykin's body, it was obvious she was dead. I was tempted to pull it back from the oven but I was transfixed when I heard what I thought was a baby crying in the living room. I went from the kitchen into the living room and was dumb-founded to see this little mite – a tiny baby boy – lying in blood and afterbirth and still obviously alive. Thank God the ambulance men arrived only seconds later and they swathed the child and applied oxygen, it was a miracle that he was still breathing and fighting for life. They rushed him off to hospital, don't even know if he's survived – it will be another miracle if he has.'

The detective screwed up his eyes and ran the nail of his left thumb through the gap in his lower front teeth – it helped his concentration. 'And then?'

'Then a second ambulance arrived and both ambulance men came into the kitchen. I don't know whether I did right

Inspector, but I just thought there was something generally wrong about everything. I asked them to hang on before they moved the body until I could get Sergeant Pollard over. The sarge was here soon after and we stopped the doctor and nurse moving the body although they agreed there was nothing they could do anyway. The sergeant rang the office to discuss the position and now you're here of course, Inspector.'

Maddox looked around the kitchen pensively. He had witnessed many a crime scene and many other horrible scenes at accident sites where fires had destroyed property and sometimes lives. This was as bad as it got. The detective asked for everyone apart from the police sergeant and police constable to wait outside a little while longer. They did. The detective looked at the door between the kitchen and the living room, then at the cooker, then at the body, at the blood stains on the floor and then the body again. Something was not right. Maddox cupped his chin in his left hand and stroked his right cheek with his index finger, deep in thought. He looked at the body again; the hands and arms were covered in dried blood.

'What are you thinking Brian?' asked Pollard.

'I'm thinking something's amiss Pete, something is very much amiss.'

'Why do you say that?'

'Well, look at the woman's hands, what do you see?' said the inspector.

'Well they're covered in blood. Hands, palms, fingers, thumbs – they're absolutely covered in blood – dried blood.'

The young constable interjected. 'Well she'd given birth alone, here, all by herself, God knows how on earth she did it but that's got to be the birth blood – what an awful experience for anybody to go through. She's given birth, crawled here into the kitchen and done herself in – what a pitiful frame of mind she must have been in – poor sod.'

'So she's committed suicide has she lad? Certain of that are you?' taunted Maddox.

'As sure as I can be, sir,' responded the young constable, now somewhat hesitatingly.

'Look at the interconnecting door,' said Maddox, 'any marks on it?'

'No, sir.'

'Any blood on it?'

'No sir.'

'No blood on the door?'

'What colour's the cooker, Constable?' continued Maddox.

'It's white enamel inspector, why?' said Stevenson.

'And the gas knobs?'

'White enamel again, with a little black arrow as a pointer and numbers,' the constable focussed closer, 'numbers one to five on each knob, settings for different gas levels.'

'And the oven knob?' asked Maddox.

'The same.'

'Which one for the oven?' asked the detective.

'The one on the right, says "oven" underneath.'

'And?' said the detective.

The constable looked again. 'Don't know what you are getting at, Inspector.'

'And?' repeated the detective.

The constable looked again. 'Just a minute. The knob is as clean as a new pin. Her hands are covered in blood.'

'It's a start,' said the inspector, 'anything else doesn't look right? Look at her head.'

'It's between two of the oven support shelves,' said the constable.

'And?'

The constable looked at the body again and then at the inspector – 'It looks unusual, sir, her head's been forced between those shelves – that would have hurt, her head's been rammed there with some force.'

The inspector looked at the sergeant with half a wink. 'I think we're going to make a bit of a detective of him one day, Sarge,' said Maddox, 'and you're right, the poor woman's been thrust into this oven with some force son – I'm willing to bet she's been murdered.'

CHAPTER SIXTEEN

Forensics were unable to find any other significant evidence at the scene to point to there having been a suspected murder. Fingerprints were weak, smudged and unhelpful. There was a melee of bloodied footprints both in the kitchen and living room where those from the authorities had gained access and done what they could. Items lying about were either domestic or had been left by the ambulance personnel as they did their morbid duty. The rest of the house had been searched from top to bottom; there was nothing untoward. The body of Lily Daykin had been conveyed to the mortuary where a post-mortem revealed that there was no signs of bruising and that she had died from carbon monoxide poisoning. The preliminary post-mortem report was with the police the following morning.

Brian Maddox was convinced it had been murder. He had arranged to delay the house being cleaned up and he wanted to see it again. He decided to rendezvous there at 3.00pm with his colleague Sergeant Peter Pollard and with young Constable John Stevenson.

'No blood or clear fingerprints on the middle door; no blood or clear fingerprints on the cooker oven switch; no blood or clear fingerprints on the oven handle, and yet I'm convinced her head had been forced between those two oven grills – there is definitely something not right about all this,' repeated Maddox.

'She died of carbon monoxide poisoning Brian,' responded the sergeant, 'maybe she did commit suicide. Perhaps it's just a coincidence that we are not finding blood where we expect it to be, perhaps she was so distraught she forcibly shoved her head into the oven in some last ditch violent act of despair. We might never get to the bottom of this.'

The detective was puzzled.

'How far have we got in speaking to neighbours, Pete?'

'Constable?' The sergeant turned to the young policemen.

'We've spoken to all the neighbours Sarge, none of them have seen anything suspicious. We've hit a brick wall.'

'What about Mrs. Lacey next door, John, surely she must have heard something? Lily Daykin gave birth for God's sake, she must have been in agony – surely there must have been screaming or shouts for help?'

'According to Mrs. Lacey,' responded the constable, 'she heard nothing. She had heard Lily arrive home just before midnight and then went up to her bed, read her library book for about another fifteen minutes and then fell asleep. She never heard another thing and didn't know anything was wrong until she came round here the following morning and discovered the body.'

'All this seems bloody impossible to me – bloody impossible – we have an emergency birth and a murder in a small hamlet like this and nobody knows anything – there's something going on here we don't know about Pete – something we're missing…' He paused and screwed up his eyes, 'But I'll get to the bottom of this if it fucking kills me.' The detective was angry.

CHAPTER SEVENTEEN

It was the back end of September, the nights were drawing in but the evenings remained mainly fine and occasionally sublime. The hamlet of Strelley Grange continued to nestle among the surrounding farmland as though nothing had happened to change the inertia of its tranquillity. But it had – forever. The murder of a collier at the local mine followed by the death of his secret lover in very suspicious circumstances had taken place – all within the last six months. And the circumstances were even more compounded. Richard Daykin had been hung until dead within the precincts of Nottingham Prison on a beautiful May morning just four months ago for the murder of Joey Murphy. And a little boy, born prematurely to Lily Daykin on the night of her murder, had survived against all the odds in Nottingham General Hospital and was now in care with a young couple living some six miles away in Kimberley. The police remained perplexed about the circumstances surrounding Lily Daykin's death – hamstrung by the lack of forensic evidence and any witnesses.

It was darts night at the Black Swan. The team from the Jolly Colliers pub in Strelley village were late but they all meandered in just after eight o' clock. They were already slightly on the merry side having downed two or three pints before leaving the Colliers.

The Black Swan livened up; it was going to be a good night. The opposing players got themselves sorted out into seven pairs – Brian Draper would be first on with Jack Creswell. Brian Smith, Mary Murphy's bother, would be the last on with Dennis Chadwick. The pub continued to fill, there was laughter and dominos, and a couple of card schools, one in each corner of the tap room. There were cheese and onion sandwiches on the side and a smell of spilt brown ale on the bar and on the quarry-tiled floor. Parents sitting at tables outside started to gather up their kids as the evening's chill started to build. The last dregs of lemonade were sucked noisily through paper straws and crisp packets were tipped to mouths for the last crumbs before walks back home.

It was now ten o' clock and the game was running at three-all with the last pair to play. Brian Smith was to lead. It was a close game; a bit of tension was creeping in. Now for the kill; double sixteen would see Brian win and the full match won for the Black Swan. He drew his right arm back, there was a transfer of weight forward, right hand back and then – an almighty cough from Brian's right rear. The dart left Brian's hand in a startled jerk; it missed its target by a mile.

'You bastard, you did that on purpose,' Brian snarled at Jack Creswell.

'Don't be mardy, Brian, that was a pathetic shot.'

The response startled everyone in the pub. Without a flicker of hesitation Smith lashed out at his tormentor with unbelievable violence. An immediate fractured jaw, a fall backwards, blood everywhere – and then he kicked the prostrate Creswell like a demented animal. There were screams, fractured ribs, a broken arm, a smother of bruises. What seemed like an eternity manifested into a rush by half a dozen men grabbing Smith and wrenching him backwards and on to the floor. He was foaming at the mouth.

'For God's sake, Brian, what on earth's got into you? You'll kill the poor bastard!'

'You're fucking right I will – he's nothing but a bastard cheat.'

'It's a game of darts, Brian, for fuck's sake – calm down. And somebody send for an ambulance quick.' Brian Draper was trying to induce calm.

'And the police.'

'No. Not the police.' It was a landlord's plea. 'We'll all be in enough trouble as it is without the police getting involved.' Geoff Davies was desperate. 'All of you, get Brian into the back room. Jack – are you alright son? Don't worry lad – the ambulance is on its way.'

Jack Creswell was released from hospital after three days. Nearly everyone knew what had happened, except for the police.

CHAPTER EIGHTEEN

The cottage was double-fronted and stood at the fringes of the main village. It was just around a corner away from the flow of the main traffic. A stark concrete road passed in front of the cottage. About one hundred yards further on, the road subsequently narrowed to a farm-track width, still suitable for tractors and heavy vehicles. There was little frontage to the cottage but behind was a large garden beautifully laid out with a lawn and beds and a sizeable vegetable plot at the very far end.

Terry and Margaret Smith had entered into buying the cottage thirty years before using an old-fashioned endowment insurance scheme. The policy had matured five years ago, paying off the capital outstanding and leaving them with over £300 pounds in the bank. In comparative terms, the Smith's had a better property than most of their working class neighbourhood and a few more quid in the bank.

Blessed with a son and two daughters, the Smiths had lived a relatively good life, being very much part of the community and of the local church. At sixty-eight years of age, Terry was still fit and well, still slim and active and benefitting from his thirty-five years as a milkman. As he got older, Terry had been surprised and somewhat disappointed that Brian hadn't wanted to be involved in his little business and preferred to stay at the pit where he had started at fifteen years of age. He often mused to himself, *Why on earth would anybody want to spend their working lives down in a dark, hot, god-forsaken place like a pit when they could be out in the fresh air and the sunshine – God only knows?* Brian was now forty-four, had never been married, never left home and after twenty-nine years in the pit looked as though he would be there for life.

Ten years into their marriage, a daughter, Mary, had come along; one of the greatest joys of their life. Then a doubling of the joy when, two years later, Tess appeared rather unexpectedly. As the years went by, there was further icing on the cake; Mary had met one of Brian's best pit mates, Joey Murphy – five years younger than Brian but like a brother – a second son to Margaret and Terry. Then a marriage, a son-in-law to die for and two beautiful grandsons. Life hadn't got much better than it was, and through it all, the rock of the family, Margaret Smith, was always there in the background for her husband, their kids and now their grandkids.

And then disaster had struck, as though God had decided to balance things up. He had decided that it wasn't fair for this family to have all the luck and good fortune. He would hit them with both barrels; a beautiful son-in-law would be proven to have been an adulterer to their daughter, he would be murdered by a jealous ex-husband, he would break the idyllic cycle and leave a whole family now decapitated, destroyed and oh so, so woefully sad. Margaret and Terry would never get over it. Although they showed brave faces to the outside world and particularly to their immediate family and especially Mary and the boys, there were heavy hearts inside that would never go away and in which they would carry their inner misery to the grave.

Terry was out back in the garden and Margaret was preparing lunch – just a sandwich – there'd be a hot meal to come at tea-time. The front door opened. It was Mary.

'Hi Mum, it's me.'

Margaret's face lit up. 'Come in sweetheart.' She gave her precious daughter a welcoming kiss on the cheek. 'I'll call your dad, he's out the back.' She rushed to the open back door. 'Terry it's our Mary.' Terry was in like a shot, a kiss, a hug, a squeeze – the sort that only fathers give to daughters.

'How are you lass? You're looking well.'

'I'm alright Dad, and how are you both?' The tone was not altogether convincing.

'We're fine, are the boys at school – are they both OK?' Margaret needed to know about her grandsons.

'They're fine Mum. It's amazing how they've coped since they lost their dad – brave boys.'

The boys had indeed been brave, but there was a shred of laboured bravery in Mary's voice – her parents knew immediately.

'Mary, is there something the matter?' Margaret had never failed to recognise concern in her three children, never, not since any of them had been born, not even now when all three were mature adults, never.

Mary hesitated. 'Is Brian at work?'

'Of course he's at work!' Already there was slight alarm in Margaret's voice. 'Why do you ask?'

More hesitation. 'Did you hear about the fight in the Black Swan last Friday night?'

'Fight, what fight?' Her father was concerned, he always panicked when violence was mentioned, particularly in the context that someone close might be involved. 'We haven't heard about any fight have we Margaret – you've not heard anything have you?'

'No.' It wasn't a convincing "no".

'Margaret?'

'Not really.'

'Margaret?'

'Mum, you do know something.' Mary was surprised.

'For God's sake. Will somebody tell me what's going on here, what is it, who are we talking about?' Terry was already fearful.

Margaret looked painfully at her daughter. Mary slowly reacted. 'Brian, Dad, Brian was involved in a fight – didn't he tell you?'

'Of course he didn't tell me.' A pause, an angry pause. 'He's obviously told you.' Terry looked at his wife

Margaret lowered her head. She had never kept secrets from her husband before, not about important matters at least, not about important matters concerning their family, not until this time – turmoil.

'So?' Terry was expecting an explanation. 'So?' The women stayed quiet. 'For Christ's sake, isn't one of you going to put me out of my misery – Christ – I don't deserve this.' He was right.

'Dad, I didn't know myself until last night, a neighbour told me. That's why I've come round. I knew that if you knew, you would be upset – and I knew that if you didn't know, I might have to tell you. I've been deliberating all night – fighting with my conscience. I first thought that if you didn't know, it might be better all round. Then I thought, well you are going to get to know anyway.'

'What do you mean – anyway?' Margaret looked even more anxious.

'The police?' said Mary.

'What do you mean, the police?' asked Margaret. Brian said the police didn't know, everybody had kept quiet. 'The police don't know.'

'They do now Mum. Jack Creswell has gone to the police – they're calling it grievous bodily harm.'

Terry Smith was welling up with anger, distress and incredulity. Something like this had never happened before in his family. In all of his sixty-eight years, he had never been in trouble with the police, neither had his immediate family, or his brothers or sisters, or his mother and father – nobody. And why had Margaret not told him? They didn't keep secrets from each other, it was not their style; their marriage had been based on trust, not secrets or lies.

'Why didn't you tell me Margaret? Why?'

'I was frightened to tell you, Terry, frightened.'

'Frightened, frightened?' the husband was now incensed. 'Have I ever, ever given you cause to be frightened of me all the time I have known you, have I, have I?'

'No.'

'Then why now, why?'

'Terry, I'm sorry, I didn't mean to keep this from you.' She hesitated. 'You know how much Brian has been upset since Joey died. They were like brothers. You know he's had mood swings, he's not himself. This is all out of character.'

'But you should have told me. He's been a pain in the backside to live with in recent months – I know you didn't know Mary – we haven't told you. He's been bloody awful –

110

and worse – Mum obviously hasn't told you – he lashed out at me two weeks ago.'

'What?' Mary was shocked.

Terry was getting angrier. He looked at his wife. 'So you haven't told her then? You haven't told her about her brother's behaviour of late and you haven't told me about his violence at the pub. What do I count for in this bloody family – nothing? Have I worked my balls off all these years to keep you all and give you everything you've ever wanted – to be lied to?' Terry was losing it. 'Have I not brought all my kids up to be respectful and honest and to carry themselves with some dignity in this bloody neighbourhood? Haven't I? Is this what it's all been for, is it? God help me.'

Mary had never seen her father like this before or her mother in such distress.

'Mum, what on earth are we going to do – what will happen to my brother?'

Before her mother could speak, her father interjected – tragically.

'Your brother?' a premeditated pause and then screaming, 'Your brother – he's not your brother – he's your fucking half-brother – he doesn't have one ounce of my fucking blood in him. His dad was a nutter. He killed a bloke in a fight on a canal bank. They sent him to prison for manslaughter, should have been murder. In any event, it didn't matter in the end, the swine hung himself in prison! It sounds to me as though your half-brother has got the same fucking temper as his wicked father.'

Margaret Smith collapsed in a heap in front of her foaming husband and her poleaxed daughter.

Chapter Nineteen

The Victorian building stood impressively on Ilkeston market place. The front door had an officious lustre to it. The oak grain spoke of some formality and it was complemented by a large brass plate on the wall to the right – it was engraved "Robinsons (Solicitors)". On the wall to the left of the door was another more modern notice giving the "Opening Hours" and an instruction – "Please ring and wait". Mary looked anxiously at her sister Tess, who gave a slight nod of approval and a tiny gesture of support and encouragement. The bell rang with energetic shrill. There was a pause and then the door partly opened and a face appeared.

'Yes?' The voice was almost challenging, it complemented the grey and dour exterior of Emily Baxter.

Mary hesitated, 'We're – sorry, I've come to see Mr. Robinson please.'

'There is no Mr. Robinson.'

'But it says Robinson on the door.'

'I know what it says on the door, that's just a name, it's historical. It's Mr. Brown that practices from here – and you'll need an appointment.' Emily Baxter could not have been colder.

'An appointment? Oh! I'm sorry.'

'Yes, this is a solicitors not a corner shop, Mr. Brown only sees people by appointment.'

'But I just wondered if…'

'By appointment only – do you want an appointment?'

'Well – yes…'

'Then come back tomorrow and I will look at the diary, tomorrow 4.00pm, and we'll try to sort out an appointment – Mr. Brown is very busy.'

There was a man's voice at the back, 'Who's there Mrs. Baxter?'

'No one.'

'I thought I heard the bell go and voices, a female voice.'

'Oh, it's this lady, says she will come back tomorrow Mr. Brown and we can sort an appointment out then.' Emily Baxter relayed the message without fully opening the door – she was shielding her little reception domain to herself – it was one of the few vestiges of authority she had over clients. Why such authority needed to be acquired was a question that only a doctor's receptionist might answer.

Charles Brown was a kind man. He had a kind face, a kind smile and, most importantly of all, a kind heart. He looked at his watch – 11.00am. 'Let me see… I've completed my work on the Wilkinson case much earlier than expected – I've got an hour to fill in – please let the lady in Mrs. Baxter.' Baxter gritted her teeth and pulled the door open with arm-bending reservation. The two women walked into the dour reception room, their beautiful but reserved presence contrasting harshly with the room itself and the greyness of Mrs. Baxter's exterior and interior.

'Ah! There are two of you?' The solicitor was obviously taken aback by the sight of Mary and Tess.

'Yes, Mr. Brown, I'm Mary Murphy and this is my sister Tess Smith.'

'Please come through ladies, and Mrs. Baxter – three teas if you would please.'

Baxter's authority had now been fully torpedoed.

The office was formal with a mahogany desk and wood-grained floor. Mr. Brown's chair exuded a sort of authority of its own, green leather – well-worn now but still exhibiting an expensive demeanour. There was a small leaded fireplace to the back wall with a colourful tiled surround. There was a small mature fire flickering away and this provided comforting warmth against an autumn chill outside. There were legal files stacked on the right of the desk, and on two tables to the sides and in both rear corners of the room. The age of some of the files gave rise to the slightest of musty smells, quietly distinct but not offensive. The wallpaper was ageing but expensive and a brass electric light fitting hung from the centre of the ceiling.

Some pleasantries were exchanged and within five minutes Mrs. Baxter arrived with a stiffened exterior and coldly placed a tray on the table – she turned and left without smile or acknowledgement. Mr. Brown served the tea obligingly.

'Now ladies, to business, what is it I can do for you?'

'It's a baby boy, Mr. Brown, presently being fostered by a couple in Kimberly. I want him.'

'You will have to expand Mrs. Murphy, please tell me where you are coming from.'

'Mr. Brown, my husband was Joey Murphy, he was a collier at Oakwood Hills colliery – you may recall, the collier who was murdered last February.'

'Indeed I do remember, what a sad case, I am so sorry for both of you.' There was a respectful pause. 'But what of this baby boy – who is he?'

'He's my husband's son, born out of an adulterous relationship with a whore, who, as I'm sure you know, Mr. Brown, died under suspicious circumstances herself – still, at least she cannot destroy anyone else's life.' There was an unfamiliar harshness to Mary's outpouring, coupled with an incongruous watering of the eyes; a paradox of emotions. A pause, a few seconds of quietness – 'But he's still the half-brother to my two sons, they carry the same blood, I want him.'

'Mrs. Murphy, I must tell you, this sounds a complicated matter to me.'

'Why?'

'Forgive me Mrs. Murphy, I do not wish to offend, how do we know this is your husband's child?'

'What do you mean – of course it's my husband's child – he was having sexual relations with her – I know – she told me herself. Furthermore, the whore has no family – her parents are dead, no brothers or sisters, no cousins, nothing.'

'But what if she was having sexual relations with another man – or other men – how do we know this was not the case? And you know Mrs. Murphy, medical tests are still not able to determine genetic certainty. The situation raises very complex legal matters, the issues are numerous, and I must tell you in all honesty, they could be lengthy and, unfortunately, expensive.'

'I want that boy.'

'Mrs. Murphy, I do not want to tell you that I will not

represent you and would not pursue matters to the best of my ability – but again – these matters could be complicated, lengthy, expensive and, Mrs. Murphy, emotionally very very painful – for all concerned.'

'Mr. Brown, I want that boy, I hate what my husband did to me, I will never, never get over it – but the nearest blood relations to that boy are my own sons. For their sake, despite what their father turned out to be, they deserve to know their half-brother and they deserve to grow up together as brothers – I am prepared to do that.'

'In many ways, I admire your magnanimity on this issue Mrs. Murphy, and I will not be so adamant as to say that I will not represent you – but only after you have gone home, thought about these matters more deeply and then to be absolutely sure what all this will mean for you and your family. Please take a few more weeks to think about things, discuss them with your mother and father and your sister and then come back to me only when you are certain in your head and in your heart that this is in the best interests of yourself, your sons and the baby in question. Please do this for me Mrs. Murphy, please take my advice.'

Tess placed her hand onto Mary's – a sisterly, comforting hand; a pleading hand.

'Mary, I think Mr. Brown is giving you the best advice at this time, you need to think about all the implications a little bit more. Mary, do as Mr. Brown advises.'

Mary stared at the desk – it could have been a million miles away – her eyes glazed, watery, sad, distant – her beautiful face ravaged with torment and confusion. A clocked ticked loudly on the mantlepiece for what seemed like an age.

'OK,' she uttered slowly and despairingly. 'Thank you Mr. Brown, I'll see you in a few weeks' time.'

The ladies stood up from their chairs, courteously, dignified. Mr. Brown shot to his feet, the gentleman that he was. 'I'll see you out personally ladies, I am so sorry for the predicament that you are in Mrs. Murphy and so sorry for what has befallen you over the past months – may God bless you both.' The solicitor led the way through reception, opened the front door, lowered his head, raised his right arm almost horizontally and guided the ladies out onto the street.

'See you in due course, Mr. Brown – we'll ring for an appointment – thank you very much.'

The solicitor lowered his head again, trying respectfully to hide his worried demeanour.

The two sisters arrived at their parents' house. It was 3.45pm. Their mother had fetched the two boys from school. As the sisters went to the side entrance of the house, they could hear the boys playing football with their grandfather on the rear lawn – the score was 7-6 apparently to Nottingham Forest – it was critical that they beat their hated neighbours Derby County, otherwise life as they knew it would come to an end. Grandad was a breathless Derby County – he caught sight of his two daughters which gave him an excuse to hear the final whistle and accept defeat with magnanimity.

The boys started a second match with unlimited lung power while their panting grandfather kissed each daughter on the cheek and entered the house with them into the kitchen. Brian had returned from the pit and was already eating his hot dinner at the kitchen table. It was a ritual he had pursued, thanks to his mother, every single day when he came home from work since the day he started. Mrs. Smith's eyes lit up in seeing her daughters. 'How have you gone on dears? What did the solicitor have to say?'

Mary dolefully recanted the details of the meeting, her demeanour reflecting the absence of a definitive outcome. 'Mr. Brown said that the issue was very complex, Mum – it wouldn't be easy to prove that the baby was Joey's son – if there was no proof, my claim to him would have no legal standing – and even if it was his son, it may still be the case that I have no legitimate claim over him.'

Brian looked up from the table with a questioning and surprised demeanour, 'Which baby are we talking about?'

'Well, Lily Daykin's of course.' Mary could feel there was something in the air, something was stirring in the pit of her stomach.

'Oh – that baby?' Brian went an instant colour of purple. His right arm swept violently across the table, scattering his dinner and everything else across the kitchen floor. He screamed uncontrollably. 'That baby – Joey's baby eh! – Joey's fucking baby – I see – Joey's – Joey's fucking baby – good old fucking Joey – what a wonderful fucking husband he was.' There was a deathly pause – 'SO WHAT MAKES YOU THINK IT WAS JOEY'S BABY – WHY JOEY'S – WAS JOEY THE ONLY FUCKING PERSON IN THIS WORLD FOR CHRIST SAKE – WHY DOES IT HAVE TO BE JOEY'S?' Another deathly pause. 'IT COULD BE MY BABY – MY SON – MY FLESH AND BLOOD – WHAT THE FUCK DO ANY OF YOU KNOW ANYWAY – WHY CAN'T IT BE MY BABY?' Brian dropped to his knees on the kitchen floor in demented despair.

There was a crescendo of silence from everyone else – including the two boys who were now peering in from the kitchen door entrance with innocent, panicking eyes.

CHAPTER TWENTY

It was raining heavily outside. The sky was grey and leaden. The kitchen in which she stood mirrored the greyness of the day but nothing matched the blackness within her heart or within her mind. Mary Murphy was now living in a spiral of pitiful circumstances and continuing revelations. Life had never been so depressing – how she managed to get up each day and get the boys off to school she would never know. Every fibre in her body, every thought in her mind told her to curl up and die – not to force herself out of bed, not to wake the boys from their sleep, cajole them to wash and clean their teeth, see that they were properly dressed, feed them their breakfast, check what they needed for school, be there when they came home and be at their beck and call at almost every waking moment.

She had not yet lit the fire under the copper boiler in the corner of the kitchen. This used to be her first early morning ritual. The water would normally have been boiling hot by this time in the morning and plenty warm enough even when the boys got out of bed for school. They normally would take a rinse in warm water after cleaning their teeth but this morning they complained – it was cold. This was not the Mary Murphy she once had been. There was a backlog with the washing and ironing; it hung about on kitchen tops and chair backs and on the stairs and on the bedroom floors. Things were going downhill badly. A weekly polish and clean had been missed for four weeks, the house was becoming uncared for – her mother had begun to notice – there was a looming psychological path developing leading to somewhere unknown.

As she washed the breakfast pots in near cold water she looked through the kitchen window with a distant gaze. All she could see was the neighbour's mirrored kitchen window staring back, close but out of focus – dull, drab, meaningless – one terraced house in relative poverty next to another – and another – and a street full next to another street full – next to – she was no longer sure or no longer cared. Mary had never looked on her neighbourhood like that before. Yes, everyone knew that life was hard and money was scarce but the neighbourhood was full of life and vibrancy, caring and decency, kids playing and allotment gardens sprouting and mutual respect and meaningfulness. And there had been her husband. Beautiful, in his prime, constantly smiling, teasing the boys – teasing her, grasping her secretly behind their backs – forcing himself close to her, gently but desperately, hormones flying, hands chasing all over her with a mixture of urgency and devoted tenderness. She would keep half an eye out for the boys – but willingly succumbed given half a chance – who wouldn't, knowing that what each could give to each other was beautiful unbounded passion. And then there was the love-making. In a small bedroom, in a small bed, with linoleum on the floor and cheap curtains in the window. Love-making so beautiful, so pleasurable and so

121

wonderful that the only thing that mattered was its blissful excitement and the repeated pinnacles of joy that negated the dour surroundings and replaced them with a cornfield of pleasure. No amount of money could have bought what they achieved almost every night through their physical, unrestrained, magnificent unions.

And now – unrestrained despair. Her husband murdered. His murderer, as far as the law was concerned, hung by the neck until he was dead. The murderer's wife, Joey's whore of a mistress, now having committed suicide – or was it another murder? There had been rumours flying about the neighbourhood – who in hell knew the truth? She had given birth on the night she died – a baby boy. By a miracle the boy had survived. Mary had been convinced this was Joey's boy – why should she have thought any different? Against her better judgement, she had started to make a legal claim to this baby boy – a child she had never seen – but presumed to be the half-brother of her own precious children. Was she being stupid – compounding the morbid situation she was already in? And then the bombshell, her brother – half-brother, Brian, appearing to lay some sort of claim to the child, this boy she and Brian had never seen.

And there were even more complexities to this mammoth tragedy. The only witnesses to Brian's outburst were their own mother and father and Mary herself. The boys had no meaningful comprehension of what had transpired that day. The outburst had poleaxed those present. It raised questions for her mother and father, and herself, questions that in themselves were terrifying – let alone any conceivable answers. Had Brian also been visiting Lily Daykin? Did they have a sexual relationship? Did Joey know? Did Lily's husband Richard Daykin know? Was Brian jealous of his own brother-in-law? Who else knew? Even worse – a question she almost dare not ask herself – was Brian involved in Joey's murder? He had been with Joey all that fateful day right up until the end of the shift. Were they walking out of the mine together? Was Brian in front or behind? Did Joey really go back towards the coal face to retrieve his water bottle or was it all a pack of concocted lies? Or did Richard Daykin actually kill Joey after all and hence all her questions were a fantasy of her own demented mind?

And what was the family to do now? Should they go to the police? Her father was the most decent, law-abiding man she had ever met in her life – what on earth could be going through his mind? Brian wasn't his birth son, he had taken him on when he married her mother – knowing what he knew now, would the loyalty to his difficult and possibly culpable stepson outweigh his own strict principles and morality?

All life was a tragic mess.

Chapter Twenty-One

The police had hit a brick wall on the murder of Lily Daykin. All the neighbours had been interviewed and re-interviewed. Geoff Davies, landlord at the Black Swan, where Lily had done occasional cleaning, and all his staff, had been questioned with no leads forthcoming. A comprehensive list of people who had engaged Lily for her needlework had been interviewed and people who had attended church with her likewise. Every single mine deputy and accompanying colliers who had been involved in inspecting Henshaw's Drift over the past five years and who had received Lily's generosity with a welcoming drink were interviewed – and not one shred of evidence emerged that could link her murder to any person or cause. There was a baffling silence.

It was six weeks after Lily Daykin's death when, at 8.00am on a beautiful October morning, the telephone rang on undermanager Geoff Dennis' desk. The caller was lucky to catch the undermanager in his office; five minutes later he would have been on his way done the pit.

'Mr. Dennis?'

'Yes.'

'It's me boss, Bill Thomas.' The overman's voice was filled with trepidation and sadness. 'We've had another fatal accident. Someone's been wrapped round the drive drums of Piper 10's main conveyor.'

Butterflies welled from the stomach of the undermanager as he tried to take in the bad news. 'Christ – who is it for God's sake?'

'We don't know.'

'What do you mean you don't know Bill – you must know.'

'Boss – we don't know – if you could see the mess here you'd understand. Whoever it is has been wrapped round the drive drums for some time, everything is mangled – there's blood, guts, brains everywhere, everything is virtually unrecognisable.'

'Has anybody been reported missing?' The undermanager was shaking.

'We're not sure yet boss – I've sent Jimmy the belt driver down to the coal face to make enquiries. I've got four day-wage men here helping me with the mess – one's a first aider but it's not first aid that's required Mr. Dennis, it's sack bags – I can't begin to describe what we're looking at here.'

Desperate quietness from the undermanager.

'I understand, Bill – we'll get some sacks and more help to you pronto – God knows what Chivers is going to say – he'll go looney. Bill, while you're working on the mess, try to see if you can find the man's cap-lamp battery or his belt with his tally on – his clocking-in number will tell us who it is.'

'OK boss – I'll let you know immediately if something shows up.'

The undermanager was in a mortified state of shock and trembling like a leaf. Any accident at the mine was treated with concern but a fatal accident always felt like a bombshell. There was an innate understanding between everybody at the mine that everyone that worked there was at extra risk by virtue of the job they were in – mining wasn't for the faint-hearted. The psychology of the occupational circumstances invoked occasional macho behaviour or bravado. There were some men who automatically took the lead when things got rough – a major fall of roof, a runaway tram smashing all to smithereens, a broken belt conveyor causing production delays or an inrush of water or gas. Mature, competent supervisors, deputies and overmen took control, or a chargeman – usually appointed for the very reason that they would respond to any crisis as a matter of norm – would also take the lead when called upon. But a fatal accident represented failure at the mine. The news would spread immediately to everyone employed there, to their families and to the wider community – the whole mining fraternity and the extended locality would be brought together in some kind of corporate grief.

The undermanager made his way to the manager's office. He knocked on the door in a state of shock and complete despair and with stomach-renching fear. He heard the usual bellow from Chivers – 'Come in.'

'Mr. Chivers,' the undermanager took in a gulp of breath, 'we've had a fatal accident underground – Bill Thomas has been on the phone – somebody's got mangled round Piper 10's belt conveyor drive – they don't know who it is as yet.'

The colliery manager went an immediate colour of purple. Aggression rose in his whole demeanour – the expected response came.

'Fuck me! What sort of mad-house are you running underground Dennis? I expect the fucking guards have been taken off or have never been fucking on – how has the twat managed to get wrapped round the rollers – and who is he anyway?'

'Mr. Chivers – the whole of the belt conveyor drive has always been guarded – and we don't know who it is that's been killed.'

'Don't know? Why the fuck don't we know?'

'Because the body is unrecognisable Mr. Chivers – according to Bill, it's in a complete mangled mess.'

'This is all we fucking need.' The colliery manager was ready to burst. 'First we have a murder underground and all the mither that brought and now a fatal accident – a fucking fatal accident. We lose coal left, right and centre – we bring a bad name on the pit – and me – we're losing money hand over fist and the owners of this fucking place are going to dump me out of a job. And – do you know what I've got to do now Dennis – you've guessed it – I've got to ring the bastard inspectorate and get those interfering twats here again to rip us apart.'

There was a knock on the manager's door. 'Who is it?' bawled the mine manager.

'It's me Mr. Chivers.' It was Ivan Johnson, the undermanager's batman.

'What the fuck do you want?' Chivers didn't want any interference from a lackey.

'It was to let Mr. Dennis know – and you know Mr. Chivers.' There was hesitation and trepidation in Ivan Johnson's voice. Bill Thomas has contacted me and he wanted you to know straight away Mr. Dennis.'

'To know what?' blurted Chivers.

'To let you know he'd found the cap-lamp of the deceased and rung the lamp-room to check who it is.'

'And?' The colliery manager screamed, his blood-red face bursting in uncontrolled temper. 'And?'

'It was check tally number 203 Mr. Chivers – it looks like it's Brian Smith that's been killed.'

CHAPTER TWENTY-TWO

Further confirmation emanated from the mine that it was Brian Smith who had been mangled in the drive drums of Piper 10's conveyor. The men undertaking the recovery had found his belt with the tally number on, it had been confirmed that he had not arrived at the coal face, where he had been deployed, and some fragments of his clothing had been recognised by his colleagues. The message of his death had quickly spread throughout the mine and all of the dayshift personnel where preparing to leave the mine in sympathy with what had happened.

By the time John Day, the training officer, had been despatched to inform Margaret and Terry Smith of the awful news, Ken Wrigley HM District Inspector was at the mine together with the coroner's officer, on this occasion Sergeant Pollard from the Ilkeston Police. Within half an hour, the investigating party comprising a locum doctor, Chivers, Wrigley, Pollard, Dennis, supervisor and workmen's inspectors and surveyors were descending down No. 1 shaft to make the two-mile journey into Piper 10's maingate roadway which housed the conveyor.

The inspection team arrived at the conveyor drive-head within three-quarters of an hour and were met by a residue of supervisors and miners. Alongside the drive-head were eight sacks of morbid, horrific, human contents. There was an unbelievable solemnity in the air and disbelieving faces on miners cornered in a surreal, unexpected and gruesome situation. One or two miners and overman Bill Thomas were still rooting about slowly, silently and painfully along and in the drive-head area and the conveyor belt tensioning loop, with sacks in their hands. They were picking up the final fragments of body scraps and clothing. There were two separate heaps of vomit in the side of the tunnel – the pitiful operation of recovery having overcome at least two of the outwardly tough miners.

Undermanager Dennis made the first approach to the overman. 'Bill – are you alright, is everybody here alright?'

'I think so boss – a couple of the guys have been really upset but we've got top side the situation – I think we've just about collected what we can,' the overman swallowed with grief. 'Poor sod, look at what's in these sacks – I can't tell you how difficult it's been Mr. Dennis.'

Colliery manager Chivers interjected in full character. 'How the fuck has he got in there Bill – were there any guards missing?' Bill Thomas looked discretely at his undermanager for silent support – undermanager Dennis gave an almost imperceptible affirmative nod. It was a signal to tell the colliery manager what he knew.

'Mr. Chivers, it was me that found him. I reckon the belt would have been started by old George from round the corner; he can't see the drive-head from round there, he can only see the coal coming down the chute and onto No. 3 trunk conveyor. He wouldn't have a clue that the accident had

130

happened. George tells me he started Piper 10's conveyor around 7.30am this morning and I got here about 7.50am on my way into the district.'

'And what did you find Mr. Thomas?' asked HM District Inspector Wrigley in his usual polite manner.

'Mr. Wrigley, it was a sound that I first noticed. It was like a slapping sound or flapping sound, it was unusual, I could hear it even over the noise of the conveyor drive motor and gearbox. I looked at the conveyor drive-head and saw that a guard was off on the hidden side where the drive drums are and it was resting on the gearbox side cover. I thought this was unusual and expected to see somebody doing something or other behind the drive-head – but there were no cap-lamp lights.'

'And?' interjected manager Chivers with an air of impatience. 'Get to the point.'

Bill Thomas looked at his undermanager again and received the same nod of quiet assurance. It wasn't enough – the overman was overcome with grief again and words were choked back with embarrassing pain. All the men within ear-shot were registering sympathetic looks for the poor overman – except Chivers, who retained an air of irritable impatience.

The overman recovered his composure. 'Then I looked where the noise was coming from. I saw something I'd never seen before – a human being – or what looked like the remnants of a human being – rolled round and round the drive drums like a rag doll. I could see the drums covered in blood and innards and clothes and brains. I tried not to panic – I don't get paid to panic. I pulled the two signal wires together and the belt conveyor stopped. I ran down to the junction and shouted to old George not to start the conveyor and to go to the panel to isolate it. I ran back to the site of the accident and could see that, whoever it was in the drive, had been mangled to bits. It's then when I rang Mr. Dennis to tell him what had happened.'

'Thank you Bill,' responded Wrigley, whose duty it was to conduct the official investigation. He addressed the inspection party. 'Gentlemen, I suggest we all have a little walk round the accident site area and see what we can see. Don't move anything else now that the body has been recovered; the surveyors need to pick up the detail just as we have found it for the purposes of evidence.'

The inspector, mine manager and mine undermanager stayed in close proximity and wandered around the conveyor drive-head. At the blind-side of the drive-head was a mesh guard about six feet long and four feet high. It was leaning against the drive-head gearbox outer shell. At the point where the guard had been removed, a large drive drum was exposed, some four feet in diameter, there was a second drive drum to its immediate rear. The belt of the conveyor was led in an "s" shape around both drums such that, as they rotated, the belt conveyor passed around them and was powered and driven with the full one hundred horsepower of the electric drive motor. As the belt conveyor fed onto the drums it formed a nip point where anyone drawn in would be squashed with unimaginable force onto the drums. It all would happen in a split second and there would be no chance of anyone extricating themselves from an instant death. This was the way poor Brian Smith had died.

'It looks as though this guard has been taken off its

hangers,' said Chivers. 'Look, the hangers are in place and the conveyor would have been guarded properly with the guard in the right place.' The colliery manager was already taking up a defensive posture to avoid any possible intimation that the guarding had been unsatisfactory – a circumstance which might have subjected him to liability and possible prosecution.

'I think you're right Mr. Chivers,' responded the inspector – much to the colliery manager's relief.

'I wonder if Brian had taken the guard off to do some cleaning out of coal fines or something – but why would he be down here doing that, I wouldn't know, he's supposed to be at the coal face, not doing a day-wage job on the conveyor.' The undermanager was puzzled.

The inspector was also perplexed. 'I don't think for one minute the guard was taken off for cleaning purposes Mr. Dennis – look – the floor around the drive-head is as clean as a new pin and – in any event – there's not a shovel in sight.'

All the members of the accident inspection party wandered around the accident area looking for some clues, some signs, some piece of equipment that would indicate why the accident had occurred. There was nothing. They looked a second time and then a third – nothing.

Eventually Chivers broke the silence. 'So what the fuck are we supposed to do now? We need to get back to some normality – we need to do a final tidy up and I need to make sure we can get this coal face back in production tomorrow when the men are back at work – we can't afford to lose another day's output.'

In reality the colliery manager was right – the accident site did not yield any additional information other than it would appear that the guard had been removed and, somehow, Brian Smith had got himself wrapped round the drive drums.

'Mr. Chivers, Sergeant Pollard, can I suggest that Bill Thomas and his men complete the final clean up and that all the sacks are transported out of the mine and on to the police forensic laboratory. I know it's morbid but examination of the remains might yield some clue or other that's not readily apparent to us here. The surveyors can then get on with their work and draw a plan up of the accident site.'

'Sounds good to me Mr. Wrigley,' responded the mine manager, 'the quicker we get back to normality the better.' The cold-hearted retort registered with everyone within earshot – but it wasn't unexpected – everyone at the pit knew that Chivers was a fat, lying, cold-hearted bullying bastard.

'Can I leave that with you Bill?' asked undermanager Dennis of the overman.

'Yes boss,' came the reply.

'And when you have completed that Bill, get the men into the canteen for a cup of tea – and a snack if they want one – and then get them off home.' The kindness and dignity of the undermanager irritated the colliery manager beyond belief – but he said nothing.

The inspection party members reported back to the conference room. The inspector reviewed what they had seen and what they had found underground in less than fifteen minutes. There were no questions – just an occasional nodding of the head and an all pervading silence.

'Thank you then gentlemen – I'll just finish off privately

with Mr. Chivers and Sergeant Pollard and then I'll get back to the office.' The men shunted quietly from the room.

When they had left, the inspector addressed Sergeant Pollard. 'Sergeant, would you be kind enough to ask your forensics to check thoroughly every stitch of clothing as well as the body parts, notwithstanding the mess that it is all in – you never know what might turn up.'

'I will indeed Inspector,' came the response, 'good day to you both.'

Immediately the sergeant left the room, Wrigley expressed his deep sorrow to the mine manager. He finished, 'Very unusual circumstances Mr. Chivers – I don't think we can do much more at this juncture other than wait to see if forensics turn up with anything… and pray for the family of course – good day.'

The bit about praying went over the mine manager's head – 'Thank you Mr. Wrigley – good day.'

Chapter Twenty-Three

Late autumn was bringing a chill to the air in the mining community on the Nottingham/Derbyshire border. The year had been unreal for the township of Ilkeston and the surrounding villages. A murder followed by a hanging followed by a fatal accident – all associated with the same mine and all afflicting or relating to the same family. The Smiths had lost a son-in-law and now, unbelievably, a son – an adopted son as far as Terry Smith was concerned. Their lives, those of their two daughters and their two grandsons had now changed forever, and a moral cloud hung over the family. Did Brian's outburst on that fateful day when he had swiped his dinner across the kitchen floor mean that he was somehow associated with the death of their son-in-law? Only Terry, Margaret and their daughters Mary and Tess knew what had happened that day and their family secret hung like a lead balloon around their necks, particularly now that Brian had died so tragically at the mine. They had not informed the police when it had first happened, fearing that the ramifications might be too unbearable, and the possible implications for Brian too terrible to contemplate. For Terry Smith in particular, the decision to hold back information, to possibly obstruct the course of justice, not to tell the truth, went against all that he stood for and believed in. But flesh and blood, albeit biologically not his in Brian, had overridden his moral compass and had left him adrift to live the life of a lie as far as what they knew and hadn't revealed. On balance, Terry was doing this for the sake of his wife, Brian's biological mother – there was no other person in the world that he would have compromised his principles for – but still it hurt and the hurt would never go away.

It had been nearly a week since the news of their son's accident. Both Terry and Margaret were operating in some sort of distorted zombie-land, trying to pretend, primarily for the sake of their daughters and grandsons, that they would see things through. The police had not come up with any suspects for Lily Daykin's suspicious death; they had hit a brick wall. But the Smiths knew that their son Brian might not only have some association with the death of their son-in-law but also with the death of Lily Daykin – but they weren't sure – and that tiny crumb of comfort was the thing that they held on to – psychologically – convincing themselves half-heartedly that Brian had had nothing to do with Joey or Lily Daykin's murder – that he was an innocent man. But they knew that their reasoning was tenuous at the best and a complete falsehood at the worst – what were they to do?

It was 11.00am in the morning. Terry and Margaret had been up since seven. They had eaten their breakfast together – a slice of toast each, it was enough, they weren't hungry. Margaret had washed the pots with a heavy heart, deeply troubled. Terry mirrored his wife's demeanour, reading the paper with an acute lack of concentration and finding reasons for not starting work either in the garden or

137

in the shed or wherever. The mental hell he was suffering constantly deterred him from doing anything constructive. He was even reluctant to play with his grandsons; their visits had become an intrusion on his inner turmoil and he was showing signs of unreasonable irritation with them. This wasn't Terry Smith. His daughters and his two grandsons were virtually everything he lived for. He didn't need telling that, together with Margaret, they represented God's greatest gifts. But the complexity and the pain that had instilled itself into the psyche of his mind as a result of what had transpired during the course of ten months had all but destroyed him.

Terry had even contemplated suicide – a condition so remote from what had previously transpired in his life, that he had felt guilty even allowing the thought to enter his mind, let alone tell anyone else, especially Margaret. She would have probably been more angry than concerned if he had spoken to her of suicide. It was not for her ever to give up on family, no matter what difficulties had ever arisen during their married life; her children and grandchildren always came first without any semblance of doubt. She existed for their well-being and wanted nothing in return. She expected no receiving for all the giving that was in her heart and for which she gave unhesitatingly and instinctively. There was no mathematical moral balance to be struck in expecting a like-for-like reciprocation for all that she did for everyone in the family. A "thank you" or a hug in true love held more value to her than any material giving. She had everything she had ever wanted and that everything comprised her family.

Terry Smith half caught a glance of two silhouettes walking down the path at the side of the house. Five seconds later, there was a knock at the kitchen door. Margaret Smith answered the door – she was startled to see a police sergeant and a lady police woman. 'Mrs. Smith?'

'Yes,' – it was a panicked reply. 'I'm Sergeant Pollard from the Ilkeston Police and this is Constable Emma Blake – we met previously at your daughter's – is your husband with you?'

'Yes, he's right here in the kitchen with me, Sergeant.'

'In that case, may we both come in to speak to you and your husband, Mrs. Smith?'

'Of course, is it about Brian?'

'Yes it is, I am acting on behalf of the coroner and he felt it necessary and important for us to speak to you before the inquest.'

'What about exactly?' asked Terry Smith.

'Mr. Smith, Mrs. Smith – I don't know how to use the right words in this situation – I'm so sorry to have to do this. You see, the coroner needs to convey to you that – well – you recognise that Brian was severely injured when he was in the accident.'

'Yes, we know that, Officer.'

'Well,' the sergeant drew a deep breath, 'we are not talking about just severe injuries.'

'What do you mean?' asked Margaret.

'Mrs. Smith – I am so very sorry – Brian is unrecognisable.'

'What do you mean unrecognisable?'

'Mr. Smith – I'm so sorry, so very sorry – I have to tell you that there is no body as such – do you understand what I am saying?'

'How can there be no body, Sergeant?' Margaret Smith

was asking one of the most horrific questions the police sergeant had ever been challenged with. The sergeant looked at Mr. Smith and pleaded silently for him to grasp onto the nightmare of his message. Terry Smith took the signal.

'Margaret, I think the sergeant is trying to convey to us that Brian was severely damaged in the accident – very damaged. Is that what you are trying to say, Sergeant?'

The sergeant answered almost apologetically. 'That's what I'm trying to say.' He looked directly at Margaret Smith –'I'm so sorry Mrs. Smith – there is no body as such for you to see, the remains are in a coffin and there would be absolutely no purpose in you seeing inside the coffin.' The sergeant transferred his gaze to Terry Smith, 'Do you understand what I'm trying to convey, sir?'

'I do, Sergeant.' Terry took his wife fully into his arms to comfort her. She sobbed quietly. This was a living nightmare, absolute distress personified. The two police averted their gaze – both with tears in their eyes. Emma Blake offered a second comforting consolation to Margaret Smith by placing a hand on her trembling shoulder. The four people in the room lingered for what seemed like an eternity as the grim message had been conveyed and now understood.

Sergeant Pollard waited a further time – to pick a moment that would be right for the circumstances. 'Mr. Smith, the coroner has also requested me to convey another matter to you – a very important matter that you and Mrs. Smith need to know before the inquest. The coroner is trying to be scrupulously open and transparent with you so that the inquest does not reveal any unpleasant surprises on the day. Can you understand the point I'm making?'

Terry Smith responded. 'I'm not sure Sergeant – do we all need to sit down?'

'I think that would be a good idea, sir.'

'Perhaps we could all do with a cup of tea – I'll make it.'

'No, I'll make it.' Margaret Smith exhibited the enduring rock that she was and had always been. She took a deep breath, 'I make tea in this house.'

Five minutes later the four were sitting round the kitchen table, tea and biscuits to hand.

'You had better let us know what else you need to tell us Sergeant – put us out of our misery.'

The sergeant looked alternately at the doleful couple sitting in front of him, and then across to Constable Blake for some kind of professional support. Although twenty-five years his junior, her comforting gaze lent some added strength to his predicament.

'Mrs. Smith, Mr. Smith – you know that there was little recognisable after Brian's accident – his body and his clothes were a complete mangled mess – I'm so sorry.'

The sergeant waited a little longer. 'But there's a note he may have left.'

'A note – what do you mean a note?' retorted Margaret Smith, 'I don't understand.'

The sergeant continued. 'Amongst Brian's mangled clothes, in what remained of his rear pit-trouser pocket was a note – forensics found it as they searched meticulously through what was left. The note's in a bad state, the original is here in this file but, because much of it is not fully legible, forensics have typed out a transcribed copy – as best as could be interpreted. The coroner wants to know if you would like to see the transcription?'

The Smiths looked at each other mournfully. 'I think we should Margaret – we need to know.'

Margaret Smith hesitated, her eyes glazing. 'If it is going to be brought up in the coroner's inquest anyway, it might be as best if we see it now Sergeant, rather than be taken by shock on the day.'

The sergeant placed the transcribed note in front of the Smiths and Terry aligned his chair to Margaret's so that they could both read it together.

"We need to meet. Police are reviewing Murphy's murder. We need to re-look at the place where he was found at the bottom of Henshaw's Drift Wednesday 7.30am – don't be late."

The Smiths held each other in agonising pain. The two police sat quietly with heads bowed. Minutes went by.

'Did you say you have the original note in that buff file, Sergeant?'

'Yes, ma'am.'

'May I just glance at it please?'

The sergeant opened the file and eased out the ruffled note carefully and laid it on the table.

The Smiths looked at the note with intent.

Almost without hesitation, Margaret raised her head and looked at the police sergeant.

'That's funny,' she said.

'Sorry ma'am?' The policeman was taken aback.

'Sergeant – I said that's funny – our Brian was almost completely illiterate and rarely wrote anything. When he did, he only ever wrote in capital letters. For your information sergeant – that is not our Brian's note – it's a note that has been sent to him.'

Chapter Twenty-Four

'Good morning, HM Inspectorate of Mines,' answered Dawn Jones.

'Hello, good morning, this is Sergeant Pollard, Ilkeston Police, presently acting as coroner's officer – is Mr. Whatmore the senior district inspector in please?'

The secretary connected the call through to Cyril Whatmore, 'Mr. Whatmore, I have Sergeant Pollard of the Ilkeston Police on the phone in his capacity as coroner's officer – you're through, Sergeant.'

'Good morning Mr. Whatmore – more surprises I'm afraid.'

'Really – what is it this time sergeant?'

'It's the accident concerning Brian Smith at Oakwood Hills colliery – we have reason to believe that there are some suspicious circumstances connected with it – there is a possibility that we might be dealing with a suicide or even a murder.'

'Really – how come sergeant?'

'Forensics found some kind of note in the back pocket of his pit-trousers – it was pretty tangled and much of it could not be deciphered. The coroner wanted his parents to see the note before the inquest inspector instead of it just appearing on the day – you know that Mr. Shaw is always keen to be sympathetic and helpful whenever he conducts an inquest.'

'A very fair man, Sergeant.'

'We took the transcription to Brian Smith's parents' home and also showed them the original note, albeit in its decrepit state. What a shock – the note is handwritten in normal letter cases – you know, capital and small letters – but it turns out that Brian was pretty much illiterate and when he did write, which was not often, he only wrote in capital letters.'

'Not wanting to jump to conclusions, Sergeant, but the incident seemed to lend itself more to an accident than suicide and surely not murder,' said Whatmore.

'Well, we're going to keep an open mind on it. It looks as though we've all got our work cut out again I'm afraid. Will you have staff available to conduct a round of interviews with us inspector? The input of your staff was invaluable when we dealt with Joey Murphy's case.'

'Of course – let us know of your requirements and we'll respond.'

'Thank you Mr. Whatmore, I'll be in touch.'

The police and the mines inspectorate took eight weeks to interview witnesses, collate statements, re-analyse circumstances and evidence taken from the scene, review forensic detail and pursue every imaginable line of enquiry. The work hit a complete brick wall with not a trace of a lead as to how and why Brian Smith had become wrapped round conveyor drive drums underground at the colliery. The source of the note could not be traced.

In the tenth week, at the inquest of Brian Smith, the coroner gave an open verdict.

The police were under pressure from the public. Even the miners at the pit – not known for their lack of fortitude – were becoming restless, after all, who was next in line? Even the Chief Constables of Derbyshire and Nottinghamshire were being harangued by local politicians and councillors to come up with some explanation as to what on earth was happening at the mine and when someone was going to be arrested.

CHAPTER TWENTY-FIVE

The brass plate that signified "Robinsons (Solicitors)" still shone as good as new. The oak grained door retained its expensive lustre and this time the sisters had made a formal appointment with Mr. Charles Brown. They rang the bell and to their surprise, as the door opened, it was not the face of Emily Baxter that greeted them but that of a charming young girl who looked about eighteen years of age. She smiled.

'Hello, is it Mrs. Murphy?'

'Yes and this is my sister Tess.'

'Please come in ladies, my name is Jennifer Cross, Mr. Brown is expecting you.'

The young lady led them to the solicitor's study, introduced them and asked if they would like a drink – tea or coffee?

Mr. Brown was his normal gentlemanly self, standing bolt upright as the ladies entered, pulling out chairs and beckoning that they sit and make themselves comfortable.

'Thank you Jennifer, I'll take my usual tea as well please.' He then proffered a warm and gentle smile to the females in his presence. 'Good morning ladies, it's a little while since I last saw you I know, how long – eight weeks?'

'Nearly ten, Mr. Brown,' responded Mary, who had been counting every day since their first meeting.

'Good Lord – as long as that?'

The wise solicitor deemed it appropriate to start with some delicate small talk. With over twenty years' experience he knew that lunging into immediate business could come across as cold, formal and overbearing. There was a need to assimilate the client, the context, the seriousness of any situation and the case being dealt with and to proceed appropriately – but before he could speak:

Mary asked, 'Is Mrs. Baxter on leave?'

'Actually she's decided to take early retirement, she'll be sorely missed.'

Both sisters gleaned that the solicitor's answer was cloaked in some professional diplomacy.

'So, how are you both? And how are your mother and father?' It was a genuine question asked with absolute sincerity.

'I think I'm as well as can be expected Mr. Brown.' It was not a statement entirely supported by the look on her sister's face. 'We got the funeral over with, which was the hardest thing I've ever done in my life. The boys miss their father terribly, that's obvious, and yet they seem to be coping somehow. I don't know whether it's the youth in them or what but they do seem to be getting on with their lives. I think having good friends has helped tremendously.'

The solicitor homed in on the positive. 'Children do seem to be remarkably resilient in many circumstances. Paradoxically, I think their natural immaturity simplifies the complexity of death and other nasty things and they seem to be able to revert to normality especially when they have friends about them.' It was an insight that the sisters understood.

'And your mother and father?'

'They are bearing up,' responded Tess. 'Well, Mother is but Dad still seems to be suffering inside terribly. I don't know whether he'll actually get over all this. He's certainly not himself by a long chalk.'

The solicitor's face expressed sympathy; it wasn't contrived.

'Sometimes life throws things at us completely out of the blue, randomly as it were. None of us wants to be in the firing line but few of us avoid some tragedy or other during the course of our lives. Those that do are extremely lucky. Of course, I see it all the time during the course of my work. Death, bereavement, divorce, accident, settlements, civil tort – you name it and we have to deal with it. But that's what we get paid for, so I shouldn't moan about it.'

The sisters listened to the wise old man respectfully but Mary was keen to get to the purpose of their visit and it showed ever so slightly on her face. The solicitor picked up on it.

'Anyway, we had better get down to business.' He took a deep breath.

'You came here, Mrs. Murphy, in the hope that you would be able to adopt the poor child that was born to Lily Daykin on the fateful night when she died in such tragic circumstances. That was some six months or so ago.'

The sisters nodded their head in the affirmative.

'Well,' Charles Brown hesitated, 'matters are complicated. I need to tell you that I've done some quiet research on everything I could in this case. I have to be very careful; on the one hand I am desperately keen to help you, on the other

I do not want to stray out of my professional boundaries – although I must admit – I have stretched things in that regard as far as I dare.'

The sisters were all ears. The solicitor was unusually hesitant – matters were delicate.

'Firstly, you see, there is no reliable medical test to prove paternity for a start. And – what should I say? My enquiries have indicated that Mrs. Daykin was – how I can I put this...'

'A whore!' There was no hesitation from Mary. The solicitor was taken aback.

'Well, I couldn't possibly use that word Mrs. Murphy – but let's put it another way. My enquiries have indicated that at least three men were enjoying Lily Daykin's company at the time your husband was involved. I'm sorry.'

'There's no need for you to be sorry in that context Mr. Brown. The whore probably got what she deserved, I blame her for enticing my husband – she was probably an expert at it. He was just an idiot.'

A moment's pause.

'So medically proving paternity is not going to be possible. Then we turn to the depth of the relationships Lily Daykin had with the respective men involved. None of us know about the detail – and maybe we will never know now that she is dead. I'm sorry Mrs. Murphy but who may have consummated what, where and when, will have died along with Lily Daykin.'

'But the child could be Joey's – the stepbrother to my own sons.'

The solicitor hesitated yet again.

'Mrs. Murphy, I can tell you that I have reason to believe that the child is almost certainly not your husband's son.'

'How the hell do you know that?'

'Mrs. Murphy – I was hoping against hope that you wouldn't ask me that. I told you that I may have reluctantly exceeded my professional boundaries in trying to help you in this case. I plead with you – please don't push me into a corner that might affect my professional standing. I simply want to make the point that if you pursued this paternity matter in court, it would be very very expensive and – even more to the point – you're almost certain to lose.'

'How can you possibly be so certain?'

'I am certain – very certain.'

A pause and silence.

'Then there is the matter of the foster parents in Kimberley,' the solicitor continued.

'What about the foster parents?'

'I have it on good authority that the foster parents are wonderful people. Apparently in their late twenties and couldn't have children themselves. They have taken to this foster baby boy as if he is their own. They are overjoyed to the extent that they are already considering pursuing legal adoption. I want you to understand, Mrs. Murphy, that the most important person in this sorry situation must be the baby and its future wellbeing.'

Mary was taking on an air of dejection. Tess held her hand. The saddest of all smiles passed between them.

'Why can't I adopt the baby?'

'Mrs. Murphy – adoption doesn't work like that. Propriety is essential and there are too many complications as far as you are concerned. Your husband was apparently involved with the child's mother, he is almost certainly not the father. You may have, with some justification, resentments of her which may carry over to the child later in life. You never know. And what about your own sons, how do you know that they themselves might not resent a stepbrother later in life? These things happen. They may even get to know about the circumstances of their own father's relationship with the mother of the child. You must understand that all this could lead off to complications, not only for the child, but for you, your own sons and even your wider family.'

'I know what you are saying Mr. Brown, but it hurts inside. The pain of this is unbearable. If I could only have the child, I know in my heart that I would always look after it.'

'I don't doubt that for one minute Mrs. Murphy, but you must be rational about this, the information and advice I am giving you is the best I can do – please accept it.'

There was no answer. The solicitor was still not convinced he had won the day and got his client to accept the inevitable. More silence. Charles Brown waited with deliberation etched on his face. He continued.

'And there is another matter.'

The sisters looked up. Tess interjected – 'What other matter, Mr. Brown?'

There was an inevitable reluctance in the demeanour of the solicitor. He wanted to remain silent but, against his better judgement, he continued.

'It appears that the child may have a life-long benefactor. It may well be the case that he will want for nothing. Whatever the rights and wrongs of this, should we, do we, have the right to deprive him of that possibility? I know money is not everything – by far – that's for certain – but who are we to determine the influences that might be brought to bear on the child for his life-long wellbeing?'

'Who is this so-called benefactor?'

'I couldn't possibly tell you that. I am already sailing very close to the wind divulging what I have already said – but I am doing this for you Mrs. Murphy, you are my direct client and believe me, I have both your finances and wellbeing as my first priority.'

Mary Murphy looked down at her knees and at her sister's hands resting on hers. She was thinking what a comfort it was to have someone at your side who really loved you without any conditions. She looked into Tess's eyes and saw the pleading of a wonderful sister. There was desperation in her eyes. Mary knew what her sister was thinking. She waited and waited. Her mind started to galvanise. She waited further and then, slowly:

'Mr. Brown – I am going to take your advice. In my heart I know that you are right and, furthermore, I know you have my interests and the interests of the child at heart. You are a really good man. I swear to you that I will never pursue this matter again.' And then, 'Tell me Mr. Brown – how much do I owe you for all you have done?'

The solicitor looked at the pitiful woman in front of him being comforted by her sister.

'Nothing, Mrs. Murphy, nothing.'

There was a considerable degree of relief showing on his kind face.

CHAPTER TWENTY-SIX

The late autumn chill was starting to set in and days were shorter and darker. The hamlet of Strelley Grange nestled dankly in its rural setting with little added human traffic other than visitors to the Black Swan – many less now than in the height of summer. The farmers had finished harvesting and were now busy starting to winter plough and trim back the hedgerows. The lanes had their fair share of leaves and mud, wet and slimy; not a problem for the tractors, but any rare visit by a motor car had to be undertaken with care. Ditches ran freely with rain water, and local streams – nearly dry in summer – ran with vigour down to the River Erewash and then on to the Trent and Humber and out into the cold North Sea.

Most of the residents were elderly and were preoccupied in keeping warm. This wasn't exactly straightforward. The coalman delivered coal in sacks and dumped it into outside coal houses. This was a bonus compared with people living in built-up areas with hard standing roads – here the coal was just tipped loose and had to be shovelled and barrowed into coal houses, requiring some considerable effort. Even so in the hamlet, coal scuttles and buckets had to be filled on a daily basis and kindling wood either purchased or collected from the countryside. On some mornings, fires had to be started from scratch with newspaper and kindling and other times, where coal slack had been mounded onto the late evening's fires, embers remained hot enough the following morning to relight the kindle and then the coal to reinvigorate a fresh fire. Ash had to be scooped from below the fire grates every morning and dumped into an ash bin outside and collected on a weekly basis.

For those that did still work in the hamlet, the usual mode of transport was by bicycle or Shank's pony.

Everyone in the hamlet kept an eye out for each other. This didn't usually entail formal and routine visits but occasional visits for cups of tea and a chat. There were other mechanisms for noting that neighbours were about and alive and kicking. Smoke from the chimneys, washing on the line, activity in the gardens, family and friends visiting from the main village and the to-ing and fro-ing of those that did work. There were no school children in the hamlet.

A young married couple had moved in to Lily Daykin's house; both of them worked. Jim Slater worked at the pit in the surface screens and Joan Slater at the hosiery factory at Ilkeston Junction – both cycled to work, come rain or come shine. The couple had been ecstatic to have been able to rent the terrace for four shillings a week – it was their first home, it gave them privacy and consequentially an opportunity for intimacy. The elderly people in the hamlet had taken a shine to them, not least because they were a handsome couple who had brought a little youthful sunlight to their surroundings.

It was Saturday afternoon and Jim had started to prepare for his first vegetable patch in the rear garden. For him, it was an exciting venture, growing your own food for the first time in your life. At this time of the year, the work only involved skimming off some of the grass and then winter digging in readiness for planting next spring. As he bobbed up and down, digging with enthusiasm, there was a call from two gardens away. It was Mrs. Brown.

'How are you Jim? You're looking very energetic.'

'I'm fine Mrs. Brown – and yourself?'

'Can't grumble, another year older, rheumatism killing me but at my age I just thank God I'm here. And how's Joan?'

'She's well, gone down to her mother's to have her bottle filled this afternoon, I'm going to join her later for a spot of tea with her mum and dad.'

Mrs. Brown smiled. 'Don't know what you youngsters would do without your mums and dads – they never stop spoiling you.'

'Tell me about it Mrs. Brown, we've both got the best parents any couple could have – don't know where we would be without them.'

'That's good, that's what life is all about. Tell me Jim, have you seen Mrs. Lacey just lately?'

'Do you know, I can't say I have but having said that, by the time I get home from work at the moment, what with the overtime I'm doing, I just dive through the front door and look forward to my hot dinner.'

'I know, I know – you youngsters work so hard – still you're fit and well and that's all that counts. God bless to you both.'

'Thank you, Mrs. Brown.'

It was now late Sunday morning and the Slaters were enjoying their day of rest as they had enjoyed their night of passion. Life was pretty good. They didn't have a bathroom but each day started by having a vertical bath in the kitchen in a large enamelled bowl placed on the floor that had been filled with warm water from the copper. The fire under the copper during the day kept the kitchen pretty much aired off but it was cold enough in the mornings in the middle of winter to induce a shiver. As Joan stood in the basin, her beautiful slim figure ladling warm water over her glistening body, Jim glanced in excited admiration while frying their breakfast. Life was very good!

'Joan, have you seen Mrs. Lacey recently – Mrs. Brown was asking yesterday?'

'No, I don't think I have. You remember she came round on Wednesday evening with those scones, haven't seen her since. Tell you what, when we've had breakfast, I'll pop round.'

Joan knocked on Mrs. Lacey's back door. There was no answer. She squeezed the door open and gave a gentle shout so as not to startle anybody. There was no response. She put her head through the door, the kitchen was cold – this was unusual, she had never been into Mrs. Lacey's kitchen when it was not either hot or at least well aired off. Perhaps she had gone out and not bothered locking the door – it was routine not to lock doors in the hamlet anyway. Joan hesitated as to what to do. She returned to her husband and they decided it might be appropriate to fetch Mrs. Brown – she and Mrs. Lacey had been neighbours for years. It was better, if anyone was to venture further into the house, that it be Mrs. Brown rather than the new neighbours.

Mrs. Brown accompanied the Slaters back to the Lacey household. The older woman led the way as she pushed the kitchen door open. 'Valerie, are you in?' There was no reply – she shivered. 'This house is cold, I can't understand that – she never goes away without letting me know.'

The trio ventured through the kitchen into the living room – still freezing cold. Mrs. Brown opened the stair door and shouted up the stairway: 'Valerie, are you there?' Silence. 'I think we had better go upstairs and have a look – she sleeps in the front bedroom.' Mrs. Brown clicked the latch on the bedroom door and pushed it open gently and tentatively. She put her head round the door. Shock horror. Lying peacefully in the bed was Mrs. Lacey, bluish in colour, looking colder than the room itself, apparently dead. The young couple were terrified; they had never witnessed anything like this before. But Mrs. Brown retained her composure, she walked to the side of the bed, touched the occupant on the forehead and then looked at the youngsters – 'She's gone I'm afraid, I had better phone for Doctor Parson.'

Dr. Parson's black saloon trundled down the lane and pulled up in front of Mrs. Brown's terraced house, the Slaters were still with her. Mrs. Brown had taken off her pinafore and brushed her hair in readiness for his arrival. 'Hello, Dr. Parson, I'm very sorry to have to contact you but you need to see Mrs. Lacey immediately.'

The doctor touched Mrs. Lacey's forehead, he felt for the heartbeat at the carotid artery, he placed his stethoscope to her chest to prove the obvious. 'Yes, she's passed away Mrs. Brown, in point of fact I think she's likely to have been dead for some time – she is rigid with rigamortis. Does she have any relations nearby?'

'No Doctor, she has only one son and he lives in Newcastle-upon-Tyne with his family. Only sees him about once a year. I don't have a contact address or telephone number for him. Will the police contact him do you think? And will you be arranging for the undertaker to come doctor?'

The doctor continued to look at the bed and its occupant with a searching gaze. He rubbed his right index finger up and down his nose and then gripped his lower lip with forefinger and thumb. He remained silent.

'Doctor, will you be arranging for the undertaker?'

'I will in due course, Mrs. Brown, but would you be kind enough to send for the police in the first instance? There is something I don't like about this and the sooner they get involved the better.'

Mrs. Brown inhaled a deep breath. She faltered, 'I will Doctor, straight away, I will – Jim, Joan – I think you had better come with me.'

It was just over an hour when the police car arrived in front of Mrs. Brown's house. Two men got out – it was Sergeant Pollard and Detective Inspector Maddox.

'I'm very sorry to keep you doctor.' The sergeant had a worried brow as he held out his hand. 'Taking into account what has happened in and around this hamlet in the last eight months, I thought I had better include Detective Inspector Maddox in all this, he's had to come over from Derby.' The detective and the doctor shook hands.

'Gentlemen, I should be grateful if you would follow me – we have a death on our hands that I would like you to see.'

The two policemen dutifully followed the doctor four doors down, into Mrs. Lacey's house and up to the bedroom.

'This is the situation I'm worried about gentlemen.' The doctor gestured with his hand towards the bed and the policemen looked forlornly at its ghostly occupant.

'You have a view, Doctor?' asked the sergeant.

'I certainly do. The face to me looks distinctly more blue than I would have expected. And look here gentlemen, on the right cheekbone, if I am not mistaken, that's a bruise.'

'What do you think Brian?' The sergeant respectfully acknowledged the detective's undoubted specialism. Brian Maddox looked at the bed and the face of Mrs. Lacey for a good minute. He walked round the bed and checked from every angle. He eventually spoke. 'I'll tell you what, my guess is that this woman has been asphyxiated with the pillows.' The sergeant shook his head with some disbelief.

'I think you're probably right about the asphyxiation Brian – but the two pillows?' the doctor was intrigued, Mrs. Lacey's head was lying on top of the two pillows.

'Look at the bottom pillow, although it's the bottom pillow, if you look closely, it has a significant indent in the middle at the top, the top pillow has been overlayed over the bottom pillow – Mrs Lacey's head was not lying on the bottom pillow when she was asleep. And look carefully at the top pillow – the left-hand bottom edge of the pillow case is curved down and under slightly. Not only that, the underside of the top pillow still has a slightly convex curvature even against the weight of Mrs. Lacey's head.'

'Bloody hell, Brian.' The sergeant was impressed.

The detective went on. 'I'll tell you what I think has happened. She's been sleeping with her head on the top of two pillows. Somebody has lifted her head up, whipped out the upper pillow, slammed her head down onto the bottom pillow and pushed the upper pillow down onto the side of her face with some force. When she expired, her head has been lifted and the top pillow slid under her head from right to left. He's lifted her head up with his left hand and slid the pillow across. If you look carefully, the left side leading end of the top pillow on the lower side has tried to tuck back slightly on itself against the direction of motion. Part of the indentation made into the lower half of the top pillow when it was being thrust down into her face from above still remains, despite the weight of her head, as it was placed back onto the two pillows. It's no wonder the poor bugger has bruising to her cheek.'

'Tell you what Brian, it's no wonder they pay you five bob a week more than me – money well spent I'd say.' The sergeant had always had a good relationship with the detective. 'Doctor, if it's OK with you, we need to get forensics down here. Can you do the necessary paperwork on the immediate death and allow us to get on with things and send for the undertaker in due course please?'

'I certainly can, best of luck with it gentlemen.'

Asphyxiation was confirmed at post-mortem. Forensics found nothing in the house; whoever had entered the house and murdered Mrs. Lacey had worn gloves and stockings. The only sign of a stranger was some mud near to the rear entrance step, where, presumably, the murderer had taken off his shoes or boots. The backyard near to the entrance was paved and the remainder of the garden had been dry-ashed to negate any digging or weeding. Around the small garden were various plant pots that Mrs. Lacey had tendered with great care with innumerable different plants throughout the year. There were no signs of footprints. At the bottom of the garden was an unstructured hedge with the green field housing the return outlet for the mine some fifty yards away.

After several weeks, the police investigation hit a complete brick wall.

CHAPTER TWENTY-SEVEN

The local and national press were buzzing. The newspapers were asking a thousand questions and even the national radio was reporting frequently on the events that surrounded Oakwood Hills Colliery, Strelley Grange hamlet, Strelley village and Ilkeston. A young miner, Joey Murphy, had been murdered underground at the colliery and a jealous divorcee hung for his death. The divorcee's former wife, Lily Daykin, had been found dead in her kitchen in an unsolved murder. Her premature baby had survived and the wife of the murdered collier, Mary Murphy, had made an unsuccessful attempt to adopt the child on the basis that the child was her husband's. Mary's brother, Brian, had been found dead underground at the mine in an apparent accident but a note in his pocket left room for possible suicide or even murder. And then, the most bizarre of all, the elderly neighbour of Lily Daykin, Mrs. Valerie Lacey, had been found suffocated in her own bed. The locals talked of nothing else and emotions were running high; people were becoming wary and some even frightened. The mine was losing production, morale was low and profits had turned to losses. If output remained below par for a few more weeks, there was a high likelihood that the mine would be closed with many local men thrown out of work.

The village hall was large. It had a high apex ceiling and a slight smell of dankness, even though a free-standing, cast iron coal-fired heater, situated right-centre, had been lit in the late afternoon by the caretaker. The fire had produced some degree of warmth against the freezing cold winter's day outside and the warmth was supplemented by eight plain dangling pendant lights that added a glow to the white painted wooden panelled walls. There were eight stark steel-framed windows with old, dark green velvet curtains that no longer pulled neatly together and there was condensation on the inner glass panels that hid pitch black darkness outside.

The public meeting had been called for 7.00pm. Two fold-up tables had been set out lengthways on the small stage at one end of the hall with six tubular canvas chairs behind them. There were eight rows of tubular seats lined up in the body of the hall. Seated on the stage, facing an audience of about forty local people and local councillors, together with members of the press and two local clergy, were Peter Spencer, Chief Constable of Derbyshire; to his left Gary Davidson, Deputy Chief Constable of Nottinghamshire; then to his right David Oxbridge, Labour MP for Derbyshire Erewash; then Peter Smith, Conservative MP Broxtowe, Nottinghamshire and finally two police secretariat.

The chief constable of Derbyshire opened the meeting. He went through the complete scenario of what had happened over the past twelve months or so in the locality, culminating in the murder of Valerie Lacey. He emphasised that at least one murderer had been identified, tried and hung for his horrific crime of killing Joey Murphy down the mine. He realised that everyone was fearful that Lily Daykin had been murdered in her prime in such appalling circumstances and acknowledged that the lack of evidence was very concerning to everyone. The death of Brian Murphy down the mine looked "for all the world" that that it had been an accident but the coroner, quite rightly, had given an "open verdict" because suicide or even murder could not be ruled out. Again, there was no concrete evidence to point either way despite all the detailed enquiries undertaken by the police and the mines inspectorate and the best that forensics could do. He acknowledged that Mrs. Lacey's death was undoubtedly murder; she had been suffocated to death in her own bed. Again, evidence was flimsy and leads were poor.

'Ladies and gentlemen,' he spoke with quiet authority, 'I know your concern and we all feel your concern, I give you my complete assurance that everything in our power is being done to get to the bottom of these awful matters. The Notts and Derby police force have expended thousands of manshifts looking into every aspect of all the deaths. Our forensic laboratories have worked hard at trying to establish clues to the causations of the murders but they have not been able to yield anything that gives us positive leads. We obviously recognise the inter-relationships of some of the people concerned but this has not led us into the whys and wherefores of exactly who is behind all this. All I can say is that we will leave no stone unturned. Our commitment is as strong now as when we started and it will not diminish. At least one man, Richard Daykin, received the full due process of the law for his callous murder of Joey Murphy. We can assure you that someone – or others, will be tracked down and taken before the courts. I ask you to bear with us until that day arrives.'

The deputy chief constable of Nottinghamshire reinforced the chief constable's statement. 'I can tell you that both forces are completely engaged in co-operating with each other to best effect and the amount of collaboration has been significant. There has been a complete exchange of information between us and absolute transparency. Mr. Brian Maddox of the Derbyshire CID has taken the lead and we in the Notts CID have lent him every support with some of our best detectives.'

The audience absorbed the statements made by the two senior officers and there was an air of quiet unease – a reluctance to ask the first question. There was riddling in the seats with irritation, annoyance and fear. The atmosphere was palpable. And then – from the back – a question that stunned everyone present. 'Why don't you admit it – you hung the wrong man.' It came from Tom Booth, collier mate of Joey Murphy – it was a bombshell.

'What exactly do you mean?' The chief constable responded. 'I don't know where you are coming from.' The senior police officer had been taken aback by the opening response.

'I've known Richard Daykin all my life, I went to school with him, I started at the pit with him and did my coal face training with him. When we were young we played in the same football team and went fishing together. He did have a bit of a temper sometimes but everyone knew it was like a bottle of pop. Straight up, straight down, no malice. He had a heart of gold. He looked after his elderly parents for years, he helped train the kids at football after school, he'd occasionally help tidy up the graveyard at the church and always took responsibility for making the village bonfire for the kids every November. This wasn't a man that would commit murder – even in a jealous rage – he was incapable of acts of violence of that nature.'

The deputy chief constable responded, 'What is your name please?'

There was some hesitancy in the response: 'My name is Tommy Booth – I still work at Oakwood Hills colliery.'

'Mr. Booth. You know that Richard Daykin's pit gloves were found in his pit locker with the blood of Joey Murphy on them. There was both strong factual and circumstantial evidence that proved Richard Daykin's guilt in a court of law. The jury found him guilty beyond all reasonable doubt. All the due processes of law were followed. There could not have been a mistake.'

Tommy Booth had gained a little more confidence. 'Well, you can say what you like – I knew him and you didn't – that's all I've got to say – you hung the wrong man.' There were unsaid murmurings of support from around the room; it was uncomfortable for those sitting at the head table.

And then, from near the front, a woman's voice. 'I think she was the root of all evil. Too upmarket for her own good she was.' It sounded like a touch of female jealousy.

'I'm sorry, madam, who are you speaking about please?' The chief constable had again been taken aback.

'You should know who I mean,' came the response. 'I'm mentioning no names – if you'd have asked the right bloody questions, you might have got the right bloody answers.'

The deputy chief constable interjected with some urgency. 'Ladies and gentlemen, the purpose of this meeting was to keep you all informed and to assure you of our best intentions.

We cannot use the meeting to talk about individuals and to make accusations; this is not the correct forum. If any of you have any knowledge or evidence as to any of these deaths you must come forward and tell the police.'

'I can only support what our chief constables are saying ladies and gentlemen,' added David Oxbridge, MP. 'I know how very upsetting all this is but you must realise that the police are doing everything in their power to get to the bottom of it all. If any of you know of anything that might help them, you must bring it to their attention.' His comments were met with more irritable silence.

There were more expressions of fear and despondency. The police were further grilled about their lack of progress. The peculiar thing was that, notwithstanding all the dialogue, there seemed to be an overarching atmosphere of restraint. Even the most pointed questions were challenging but without substance; they were fundamentally rhetorical and reactionary rather than constructive. In less than an hour, the meeting was leaning towards repetition and irritability – what was intended to have been a public relations exercise had fallen at the first hurdle.

It was going to be embarrassing for the chief constable to bring such an important meeting to such an early close. It hinted at failure on the authorities' part to properly engage with those that had taken the trouble to join the meeting. On the other hand, he had gained a distinct impression that many of the people attending were there to listen to what might have been said as against to what had actually been said. Something was unreal – he couldn't fathom what it was.

Having quietly consulted other members on the head

table, the chief constable took in a deep breath to conclude the meeting somewhat unavoidably with some summary remarks that he could formulate, albeit they would be feeble under the circumstances. Before he had time to speak, the entrance door to the rear unexpectedly opened and two members of the constabulary entered with grim faces. They both made their way to the head table and the two senior chiefs sitting there. There was a whispered message. The faces of the two chiefs coloured with shock.

'Ladies and gentlemen,' said the chief constable, 'I'm very sorry, we need to leave immediately… I don't know how to say this… there's been another death in Strelley Grange.'

Unrestrained pandemonium.

CHAPTER TWENTY-EIGHT

The concrete track was about four yards wide. It led off from the lane through a five-bar gate, permanently tied back to a secure post with bale string. On both sides of the concrete pathway was secure barbed wire fencing. To the left of the pathway was sodden grazing land sprinkled with occasional thistles and an odd bare tree. In the distance there were rabbits nibbling and crunching dank grass devoid of much of its sustenance. To the right-hand side was a heavily ploughed field in dark brown waves with occasional tractor-wheel lines carrying inches of standing water. There were crows and magpies bobbing and squabbling about on the ploughed land, taking off in noisy alert every now and again and then returning back to the soil with a swoop and a halting hop.

The concrete track weaved gently for about 500 yards. The surface was worn in places and occasional pot holes carried free-standing water from the winter's heavy rains. There were tractor-tyre lines in silted mud, rotting leaves sprinkled here and there and occasional patches of whiter concrete where makeshift repairs had been undertaken to address deeper pot holes. At the end of the track was another five-bar gate, this time closed on its catch. On the other side of the gate was Strelley Grange Farm.

As the chief and deputy chief constables, accompanied by two aides, arrived at the farm gate in a single car, they could see, already in the farm yard, one police car, one small private car and a Land Rover. They got out of the car and one of the aides swung back the gate to the farm yard entrance and then closed it behind them with a degree of reverence – the party were not sure what they would be coming across but they knew it would involve a death. The group walked over towards the vehicles. A few chickens strutted about haphazardly and cows could be heard in a large barn to the left. There was a muffling, screeching and scratching coming from pigs in a brick-built pigsty off to the right. To the front of the double-fronted farm house, at the entrance to the porch-way, lay an English border collie. There was an eerie strangeness. Instead of yapping its head off at the visitors, the dog was lying down with its muzzle between its front paws in a forlorn, disconsolate manner.

The arrival of the car had been heard. From around the left-hand side of the farmhouse there appeared the figure of Sergeant Pollard. He was the epitome of disconsolateness. He made his way directly to the seniors. A dip of the head.

'Chief Constable,' and then to the others, 'good afternoon gentlemen.' The sergeant took a deep intake of breath. 'I'm afraid we have another death on our hands – at first sight it looks like an accident – would you like to follow me.'

The four men followed in a line down the left-hand side of the farmhouse where there was an open concrete yard extending to further outbuildings then to fields beyond. In the far left corner of the yard was a blue tractor with an awaiting ambulance to the side. There were two ambulance men waiting patiently. Immediately to the side of the tractor were Inspector Brian Maddox, a police photographer and two from forensics. Measurements and photographs were being taken.

'Sir, this is Inspector Brian Maddox, these people are from forensics and this ambulance is from the Derby Royal Infirmary. You'd better take a look – I'm afraid it's not a pretty sight.'

Peter Spencer moved forward with the others in his entourage following him. There was a look and then a pause. 'Christ.'

The sight was horrific. Just to the back of the tractor's rear left-hand wheel was a body. The legs were untouched but from the hips to the neck the body had been squashed thin, with tyre indentations tracked across it in the gore of innards which had flirted in every direction – red and brown and pink. Remarkably, the head was untouched but the upturned face was grimaced as a result of excruciating pain. The newly arrived stood open-mouthed in a moment of silent disbelief.

And then Deputy Chief Constable Davison asked, 'What do you think has happened inspector?'

'Sir, at this stage it looks to me like an accident but I do not want to be seen as jumping to conclusions. The tractor handbrake has not been applied. As you can see, the rear tyre of the tractor has a puncture, it's as flat as a pancake. At first sight, it appears that the guy has dismounted from the tractor to investigate and it's moved forward just as he has reached the ground. Don't know whether you can see but there is the slightest of gradients down this yard in this direction but the ground goes level where the tractor is standing. Had the tractor been parked another three feet further forward this way, there might have been a good chance that it wouldn't have rolled forward at all.'

'How unlucky can you get?' It was a deep and pensive response from the Chief Constable.

'Who's it likely to be? What are your plans now, Sergeant?'

'Sir, all we can do now is let forensics do what they have to do and then these poor guys,' he gestured to the waiting ambulance men, 'will have to get the body to the forensics morgue. Brian and I will have a complete look round the farmhouse to check whether there are any other matters of relevance. We'll make further enquiries after that.'

'And do we know who it is?'

'No sir, but it shouldn't be difficult to find out. We will need formal identification but if it is the farm owner, I'm told his name is William Jones.'

'Then we'll leave you to it, gentlemen; thank you all for your efforts tonight. If you can get a summary of where we are to me via your Ilkeston desk no later than 5.00pm tomorrow please – I should be very grateful.'

'We will do our level best on that sir, we can put something together by then, goodnight to you all.'

Six weeks later, the Derby City Coroner gave a verdict of "accidental death" on farmer William Jones – there were no suspicious circumstances.

PART TWO

(May 1956)

CHAPTER TWENTY-NINE

The weather could not have been better and the evening more beautiful. May was glorifying the hamlet of Strelley Grange with all the freshness of a new beginning. Birds were busy completing their nesting or already feeding their young. Residents showed a spring in their step as though the coldness and greyness of the previous winter had been some sort of bad dream. Walkers ambled and criss-crossed the pathways, picking an occasional wild flower or a dandelion seed-head to blow upwards towards the blue sky. Lovers hugged and kissed and laughed and then taunted each other to a false argument before hugging again and laughing even louder. There was a tractor churning away in the background endlessly traversing a distant field. Sheep were nonchalantly grazing and their new breed was growing fatter by the day in readiness for their unknown fate.

A black saloon car meandered purposely through the lanes from the direction of Ilkeston, making its way through Strelley village and then on towards Strelley Grange. Although the car was unmarked, the people inside were on official business.

There was a darkness, a dullness and a sadness at No. 8

Strelley Grange. The curtains in the rear bedroom were partly closed and there was a lingering odour of impending death pervading the air. Mrs. Brown was near white in pallor and her breathing was shallow but still quietly determined. Dr. Parson and two elderly women sat by the bed watching her every movement. Occasionally she would rally for five or ten minutes and speak cogently about old times and family, what she had done in her life and what she should have done or didn't do. There were a thousand and one things to remember and some to forget. But even when she recanted the best things that had ever happened to her, there was an overlying tinge of regret in her expressions – as though, on balance, she had failed the world in what she might have said or done at some time or other in the past. The old lady occasionally sighed with a distinct irritability, as though there was some latent frustration which she would now never be able to fully overcome.

It was all a matter of time and it wouldn't be long.

In spite of her predicament and bodily weakness, Sarah Brown had demanded that a telephone call be made some three hours previously. Dr. Parson had picked up on the urgency in his patient's request and demeanour and had dutifully responded. The call was to the Ilkeston Police – a convoluted explanation was required but there was a positive response. It would take a little time to gather the requisite people together but they would be there.

There was a knock at the front door and the old lady's eyes sprung wide open in some sort of expectation, even excitement. One bedside onlooker, Mrs. Lane, jumped to her feet and scurried downstairs. She opened the door in mild curiosity and expectation.

'Please excuse us, madam, I am Sergeant Mold of Ilkeston Police, this is Detective Inspector Gray from the Derby City Police, this is Mrs. May Cohen from the social services and this young man is Paul Scholar from Kimberley. We had a phone call from Dr. Parson, apparently there is a lady that is desperate to see this young man and desperate that there is a police presence.'

'Please come in gentlemen, Mrs. Brown is upstairs with Dr. Parson and another neighbour, Mrs. Bagshaw.'

The two policemen, Mrs. Cohen and the young man entered the bedroom with quiet dignity. Their semi-hesitant gaze fell upon Mrs. Brown and quickly diverted to the doctor. The doctor responded accordingly.

'Gentlemen – Mrs. Cohen; Mrs. Brown had expressed a wish and said that she was desperate to see this young man. I'm not sure why but she insisted. I thought it appropriate that it was done through the police and social services and that's why I rang earlier on today.' The doctor lowered his voice. 'As you can see gentlemen, Mrs. Brown is not at all well and you need to be extremely gentle in your deliberations – I will help in any way I can.'

The visiting party gathered their communal thoughts. It was an unusual and tense situation that none of them had come across before. Ice was broken. 'How are you Mrs. Brown?' enquired the social worker tentatively.

The old lady returned a ghostly peer directly at May Cohen. 'As well as can be expected my dear, taking into account that I am about to meet my maker.'

Everyone was taken aback but the doctor felt obliged to speak.

'Now, now Sarah – let's not go jumping to any conclusions.'

The old lady raised the faintest of smiles.

'Doctor – how long have you known me?'

'More than thirty years I expect.'

'Thirty-two to be precise – long enough for both of us to admit to the truth. In any event, why should I mind dying – I'm eighty-six for God's sake.' A few moments of silence, Mrs. Brown closed her eyes.

And then. 'You young man, you've been brought up in Kimberley these last eighteen years haven't you?'

'Yes, ma'am.'

'And well by the looks of it.' There was a look of pride in the old face. 'Have your foster parents looked after you properly? I know that you know they're foster parents.'

'Yes, I know they are my foster parents, they brought me up for me to know that all my life, they didn't hide anything from me– and yes – they brought me up well and I regard them as my mother and father.'

'That's good.' Mrs Brown closed her eyes. More silence – a few more now slightly shallower breaths.

And then the old sunken eyes opened again slowly.

'You see young man, I know you don't know me but I know a lot about you. I have lots of connections, I've lived here all my life, done lots of charity work, have close connections with the church – and others – people that could keep me quietly informed.'

Ears were starting to burn.

'I even know what schools you've been to and where you are attending now – private schools. First Saint Benedict's, then Dorrin House and now the Nutbrook Hallam public school. I hear you've got a place at Durham University for next year, hoping to become a lawyer I understand.' A little rest. 'I know you play football for Cotmanhay United and tennis for your local club at Kimberley – you wouldn't believe what I know about you – is all what I've said correct?'

The young man swallowed. 'I certainly can't believe it ma'am, you seem to know more about me than I know myself.' Another tiny smile came across the face of the old lady. Another minute's silence with eyes closed. No one in the room felt it necessary to speak. There was no point in invoking additional dialogue that might delay or even curtail what had to be said.

'Yes,' said the old lady, more drowsily now, more pensively. 'School fees are expensive but it seems to me that the money has been well spent.' The ensemble started to listen even more intensely.

And then another question from Mrs. Brown. 'Can you see these old wizened hands boy?'

'Yes, ma'am,' he answered.

'What exactly can you see?'

'Well obviously they are a bit wrinkled ma'am.' Another hesitating response.

'A bit wrinkled – are you blind boy?' Paul Scholar lowered his head at the same instance as another weak and tiny smile engaged on the old lady's face. More silence – eyes closed.

Eyes open wide. 'Look more closely at my left hand boy.'

The boy hesitated. 'Go on, take hold of it, don't be afraid of an old lady's hand. Take hold of it and look carefully. Well – what do you see?'

'Mrs. Brown you have a webbed finger – I'm sorry.'

'Yes a webbed finger between my little finger and my ring finger – on my left hand.' It was self-evident when you looked closely and virtually impossible to see when you didn't.

'So boy, what's strange about that? Anything to say?'

The boy looked into Mrs. Brown's sunken tiring eyes and then quickly at all the other faces in the room. No one else spoke – there was a lot to be gained by listening.

'It's the same as me, ma'am. I have a webbed finger – same fingers – between by little finger and my ring finger on my left hand.' The entire room remained deathly silent in disbelief.

More quiet. Sunken eyes closed. Shallow breathing and then one large breath with eyes now wide open. 'You see son, I have something very important to tell you. Maybe the most important thing you will ever hear in your life – listen to me carefully – very carefully.'

The room was full of ears, all listening intently. There was a revelation pending.

'You see Paul Scholar – I am your grandmother – yes – me – Sarah Brown – a grandmother to Paul Scholar – you didn't know that did you?'

'Mrs. Brown – are you sure you are all right – you must be very tired – I think…'

'Inspector Gray – I am extremely tired – more tired than you will ever know.' It was an old lady's admonishment: she was entitled, she was old – she was dying.

'But Mrs. Brown – how do you know Paul is your grandson – it might be coincidence?'

'I don't think so Inspector – you see – Paul's father – my son, William Jones – you know the farmer in the accident years ago – the one who visited Lily Daykin regularly on the side, the only female I ever knew he got involved with – he too had webbed fingers in exactly the same place – you see – it's genetic, Inspector – genetic.' More disbelief. More shocked silence.

'And another thing Inspector – strictly for your information – as if proof isn't already enough – my father had webbed fingers and my grandfather. Will you be told – it's genetic – probably been like that for generations before.' The inspector accepted his reprimand. More silence with closed sunken eyes.

And then, with eyes now wide open again. 'And another thing. None of you knew Lily Daykin – except you of course Molly,' she was looking at Mrs. Lane. 'She was your mother Paul. You're her double – dark and handsome as she was dark and beautiful.'

'Yes, I know, she died giving birth to me, my foster parents told me.'

More hesitation from Mrs. Brown – there was a decision to be made about what she had to say that would hurt more than she would ever want – but it had to be made – for the sake of the boy – her grandson. All other ears were burning.

A deep, long, weary breath. 'Paul, your mother died in childbirth – that's true – but not entirely the whole truth. Your mother was murdered in the seconds after you were born.'

An interjection from Sergeant Mold. 'Yes, I remember

being told about the case. Her jealous husband was hung for it wasn't he?'

'I'm afraid you have the story all wrong, sergeant. The jealous husband, his name was Richard Daykin, was not hung for killing his wife Lily Daykin – he was hung for killing a collier called Joey Murphy. He'd found out that Joey Murphy had been seeing Lily on the quiet – he supposedly killed him underground at Oakwood Hills colliery.'

'That's right – he killed this bloke underground – didn't they find his work gloves in his locker with blood stains on them? It was an open and shut case – I remember it now.'

Mrs. Brown's sunken eyes were closed again but her dying face belied her active brain and cogent thoughts. 'Your memory is now clearer sergeant, but the story you have recanted is still inaccurate.'

'No – I'm certain. Richard Daykin killed Joey Murphy and he was hung for the murder.'

'He was certainly hung for the murder but, and it's a big but Sergeant, he didn't kill Joey Murphy.'

'But he was found guilty in a court of law, Mrs. Brown. In a court of law.'

'Yes, I know – better than you do – but Richard Daykin did not kill Joey Murphy.'

'How do you know?'

There was distant, sunken-eyed meditation on the old lady's face. Then with long deliberation, 'Because my son, William Jones, killed Joey Murphy – and I'll tell you something else – just to get everything clear – I need to be clear now as though my life depends on it – funny that – seeing as I am dying anyway – he also killed Lily Daykin.' Gridlocked silence.

'I'm sorry Mrs. Brown you're obviously very tired,' the doctor interjected.

'Dr. Parson – Peter – you have been a wonderful doctor to me for more than thirty years but your dear patronisation – and I know you mean well – must not prevent me from revealing the truth of what has actually happened – not for my sake but for this boy's sake, in fact for everyone's sake who had been affected.' The doctor was now the third to be admonished.

'But Mrs. Brown, how could you possibly know that your son William killed Joey Murphy and Lily Daykin? How could you possibly know?' enquired Inspector Gray.

A pause. 'I know William killed Joey Murphy and Lily Daykin.' There was now the saddest of looks on the old lady's face. 'And do you know why I know – can you guess? Because he told me. You see, Lily Daykin was William's bit on the side, his mistress – he'd been seeing her for years – her husband never did know, people round here keep their mouths shut – particularly when their comfort and livelihood depends upon it. You see, we, that is I, own the farm and all this land in these parts, we own all these houses in the hamlet, we even own the pub the Black Swan – the guy there is a tenant.'

The assembled company was speechless – completely thrown by the revelations they had just heard. An innocent man sent to the gallows and a middle-aged, beautiful woman gassed to death in her own oven. The policemen started taking notes – it was undignified but it was necessary. Mrs. Brown's eyes were closed.

They opened again – wrinkled, tired, sunken but with eyeballs still gleaming with cogency.

'You see, it all seems very complicated but it's not really – not when you know the full story – not when you have the full picture. I grew up on the farm with my dad, he owned the farm with Mum but she died of tuberculosis when she was only twenty-seven, I was an only child. I think if I hadn't have been there, my dad would have committed suicide after losing mum – he loved her so much. He managed the farm more or less by himself although I was brought up to help him right from being very small – for as long as I can remember really. He had occasional workers in when he was busy ploughing and harvesting but the rest of the time he struggled through.'

She continued, 'One fateful day, when I was about eighteen, a young fella from Cotmanhay came to help my dad – it was one springtime. He came on an old bike, five miles each way would you believe.'

A quiet smile of faint admiration fell upon the old lady's face.

'His name was James Jones – he was an orphan and didn't know any of his past family. My dad took to him straight away. He was hard-working, reliable and respectful. I took to him for other reasons – he was very handsome, beautiful really.' She gave a more distinct smile. 'After about six months, it was apparent to my dad that James and I had started to develop a friendly relationship. Dad didn't mind and within twelve months, the friendship became a courtship. We got engaged when I was twenty years old – you should have seen me then – not bad even if I do say so myself. James asked my dad in the proper way for his permission. As soon as I reached twenty-one, we got married – a small wedding really.' The old lady needed to rest.

And then a small tear from her right eye. 'Do you know what happened then?' Nobody did know. 'Two weeks after my wedding my father died of a heart attack; he was carrying bags of feed through to the cattle. He never did know when to stop and take a rest. Can you believe it?' There was more shaking of heads and more silence. 'The farm was left to me in Dad's will – and more surprises. Even at twenty-one, although I knew there was more to Mum and Dad's estate that met the eye, I didn't realise that they were the owners and landlords of the ten houses in Strelley Grange and they owned the pub, the Black Swan. The business side of things had been managed by accountants Elliot and Elliot in Nottingham. Mum and Dad had never spoken about the detail of what they owned.'

More rest was needed.

'My husband was a wonderful man and we had a good life together. His only downside was a fragile temper that blew up every now and again – like a bottle of pop. He was never violent to me of course but he couldn't half lose his rag if anybody else upset him. We were blessed with two sons, Ernest and William Jones, born fifteen years apart would you believe, and they both helped out on the farm as they grew up. They were good lads in many ways but they both had tempers even worse than their father's.'

A pause and another tear.

'When he was only about twenty-one years of age, Ernest hung himself in prison after he had lost his temper on a canal bank and killed a man in temper for looking at his then girlfriend. She was Margaret Osbourne who later married and became Margaret Smith – mother to Mary Smith who married Joey Murphy. But Margaret Osbourne was already pregnant with our Ernest's child and she had a little boy they called Brian who was brought up by Terry Smith, the man who eventually married her. Brian took his name but he was actually a Jones – the son of our Ernest. He was my eldest grandson.

'My husband never got over the circumstances surrounding Ernest's death; he died a sad and bitter man at the age of fifty-three with cancer of the bowel.'

The sunken eyes opened again.

'I lived with my son William on the farm and tried to help out as much as I could. William never did marry. About five years later I met a lovely man called Harry Brown. William never took to him and it caused problems between us both which later developed into bad arguments. I left the farm and came to live here in this little house with Harry. We had ten happy years together before he too died one night peacefully in his sleep. I had taken his name but we never actually did marry. William carried on working the farm and taking the profits from it. I received monies from the rest of our estate as a landlord – landlady I should say. He would come over and see me about every six weeks but we were never really close after that.' And then pensively, 'But I always loved him as a son.'

The old lady rested. The ensemble waited. Notebooks were filling.

'And then more family complications. You see William was Brian Smith's uncle but he never told him as such. But when he found out that Joey Murphy was seeing Lily Daykin, our William's mistress, behind his back, he befriended Brian. He told Brian about him being his uncle. He also told him that when I passed away and when he, William, passed away, Brian would inherit the farm and all the rest of the estate. He then told Brian that Joey Murphy was seeing Lily Daykin behind his sister Mary's back – committing adultery. Brian was incensed. They concocted a trap. Brian lured Joey Murphy into a side road at the bottom of Henshaw's Drift where William was waiting. You see, the top of Henshaw's Drift was in our field. William could enter the drift at the drop of a hat and walk down it in twenty minutes. Brian didn't have the guts to kill Joey but William did. They tried to bury Joey below ground and Brian, who had stolen Richard Daykin's work gloves a week earlier as part of the plot to incriminate him, put them in Daykin's locker when they were covered with Joey's blood. The police and the courts fell for it and Richard Daykin was hung – a miscarriage of justice if ever there was one.'

'But why didn't you tell the police, Mrs. Brown?' the inspector was irritated and perplexed.

'I know what I should have done, Inspector – but I didn't have the guts. We are talking about my only son, my own kith and kin. It was either him or Richard Daykin. Daykin was a bastard to his wife at the best of times – so I kept my trap shut – I know I shouldn't have done but I did. I wish I had told the truth – at least the other murders wouldn't have happened.'

The doctor looked at the policemen anxiously. 'What other murders Sarah? What are you talking about?'

Mrs. Brown was resting, her breathing a little shallower.

'And then he killed Brian.'

'What?' Mrs. Lane was gobsmacked.

'He found out that Brian had also started to see Lily Daykin behind his back. She told him she was pregnant and William was beside himself with temper. William told me that the whore didn't know if the baby was William's, Joey's or Brian's.'

'But if I remember correctly, Brian Smith was killed when he was wrapped round a conveyor underground?'

'Yes he was wrapped round a conveyor alright but not by accident as the inquest had found. William had told Brian that he needed to see him at the bottom of Henshaw's Drift. Someone had mentioned possible new evidence on the Daykin case and they needed to review the murder scene together. Apparently, William had sent him a note to that effect but the police never did find out who had sent it. By arrangement, Brian had slinked off from the main walkroad into Henshaw's Drift to meet William. William told me he battered Brian over the head until he was unconscious. He dragged him round the corner unseen to a conveyor drive, took off the guard and thrust him into the drive rollers where he was mangled to bits.'

'But how did William know about the conveyor drive location?' It was too much for Inspector Gray to comprehend.

Another long but shallow breath.

'Easier than you think, Inspector. Much of the mine workings are beneath our farm land. The owner of the mine has to provide us with layout plans every quarter so that we can track if the mine is causing our land any problems. Drainage and subsidence, for instance. William could see that the nearest conveyor drive head was only fifty yards from the bottom of Henshaw's Drift and when he dragged Brian's body he knew that all the colliers would be further into the mine workings on the coal face. He took a risk that no one else would be about and luck had it that there wasn't.'

'Good God.' Mrs Lane was in complete disbelief.

Shallower breathing now.

'And then there was Mrs. Lacey.'

'Oh no! Don't tell me. I pronounced death on her too – suffocated with her own pillows.' Dr. Parson was becoming unusually distraught.

'They never did connect the murder to William – but she knew too much and William knew she did. She had been in her house on the night that William went to Lily's house and saw her giving birth in the front room, not knowing whether the baby was his or Brian's or Joey's. They had a blazing row while she laboured on the floor and when the baby popped out he dragged her to the gas oven and killed her. Mrs. Lacey must have heard everything and must have been getting more and more suspicious when Brian was supposedly killed in the mine. William had to kill her to stop things coming out.'

Shallower breathing.

'And so you see Paul, now that William is dead, and I am about to die, all of this is yours – the farm, these houses, the pub, everything as far as the eye can see. It's in my will lodged with Robinsons the solicitors on Ilkeston market place. You see the senior solicitor there is Mr. Charles Brown, my Harry's son, he will soon be retiring. I told you I knew a lot of people.'

'Sarah, how could you not say anything about all this? Because he was your son? It was no excuse. So many people killed, so many lives destroyed and you remained silent all this time. You did nothing.' Dr. Parson was now drained.

Shallower breathing.

'Dr. Parson. I eventually did do something.'

'What do you mean?'

Even more shallower breathing.

'Did you know that I learned to drive a tractor when I was twelve years old? I had been brought up on a farm like I said. The farm had been in our family for generations. I was sitting in the tractor when William came back for his usual lunch in his Land Rover. William saw me and was completely perplexed. I pointed and shouted above the noise of the tractor engine to the punctured tyre. He came over to inspect. As he crouched down to see where the problem was, I could see him, close to the ground, in line with the large rear wheel. I engaged drive for a split second.'

The old lady's eyes closed yet again – tiredness – a hint of teardrops.

'I felt the impact – not a solid bounce you understand – but sufficient to know that I had done irreparable horrible damage – to my own son – my own evil son – my once precious son.'

Another long pause.

'I didn't look down. I got down from the tractor on the other side and jumped straight into my car. Later in the evening I drove to the telephone box at Strelley and phoned anonymously for an ambulance. I drove home and waited for the news. The inquest gave a verdict exactly as I had expected. All the evidence pointed to an accident. If anybody had tried to re-inflate the tyre they would have known there was no puncture. I had let the air out – not very thorough, the police sometimes. '

A very slow, very shallow breath. She turned her head slowly but distinctly to the young man sitting on the corner of her bed. She admired him with love and with pride. And then quietly but clearly, 'Look after all that you have been left Paul – you're all that I have left.'

No breathing.